FRANKLIN PARK PUBLIC LIBRARY
FRANKLIN PARK, ILL.

GREEN LANTERN

THE ANIMATED SERIES™

STONE ARCH BOOKS
a capstone imprint

STONE ARCH BOOKS™
Published in 2013
A Capstone Imprint
1710 Roe Crest Drive
North Mankato, MN 56003
www.capstonepub.com

Originally published by DC Comics in the U.S. in single magazine form as Green Lantern: The Animated Series #0.

DC Comics
1700 Broadway, New York, NY 10019
A Warner Bros. Entertainment Company

Cataloging-in-Publication Data is available at the Library of Congress website:
ISBN: 978-1-4342-4795-7 (library binding)

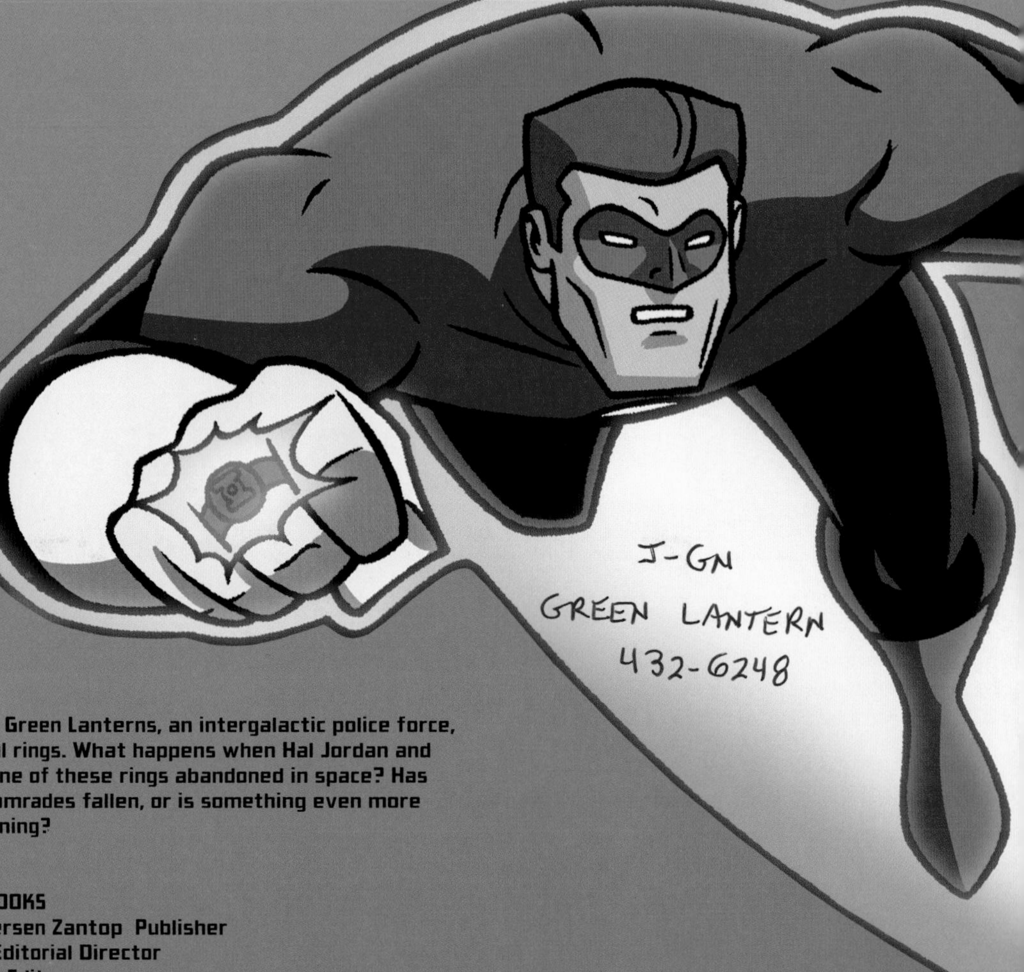

Summary: The Green Lanterns, an intergalactic police force, wield powerful rings. What happens when Hal Jordan and Kilowog find one of these rings abandoned in space? Has one of their comrades fallen, or is something even more sinister happening?

STONE ARCH BOOKS
Ashley C. Andersen Zantop Publisher
Michael Dahl Editorial Director
Donald Lemke Editor
Heather Kindseth Creative Director
Hilary Wacholz Designer
Kathy McColley Production Specialist

DC COMICS
Kristy Quinn Original U.S. Editor

Printed in China by Nordica.
0413/CA21300442
032013 007226NORDF13

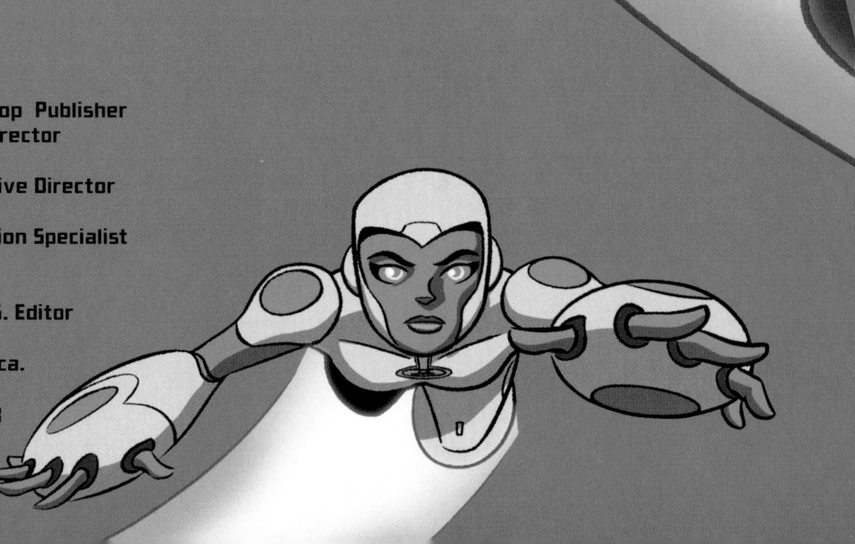

GREEN LANTERN

THE ANIMATED SERIES™

TRUE COLORS

Art Baltazar & Franco...................writers
Dario Brizuela............................ illustrator
Gabe Eltaeb & Dario Brizuela.....colorists
Saida Abbott ....letterer

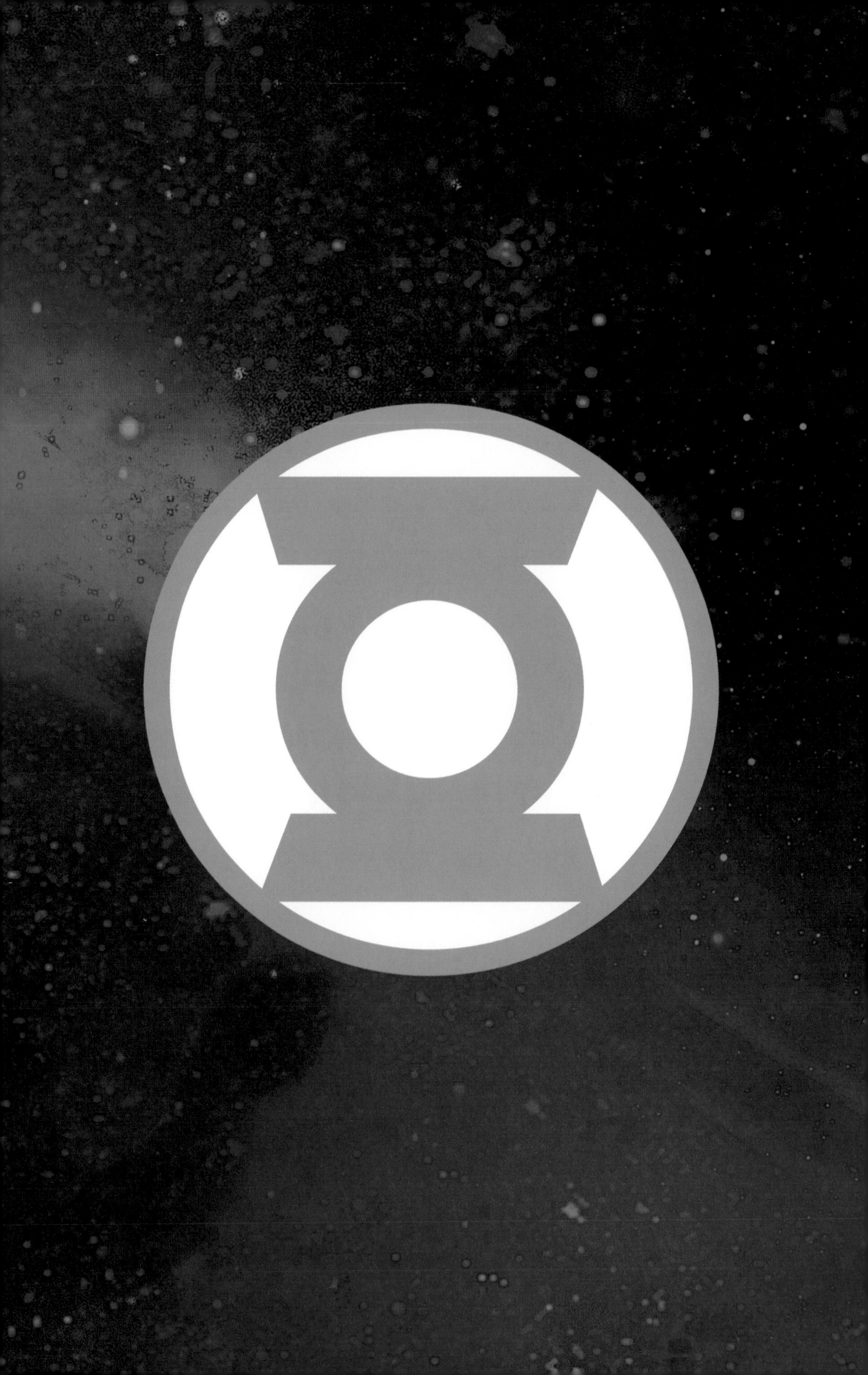

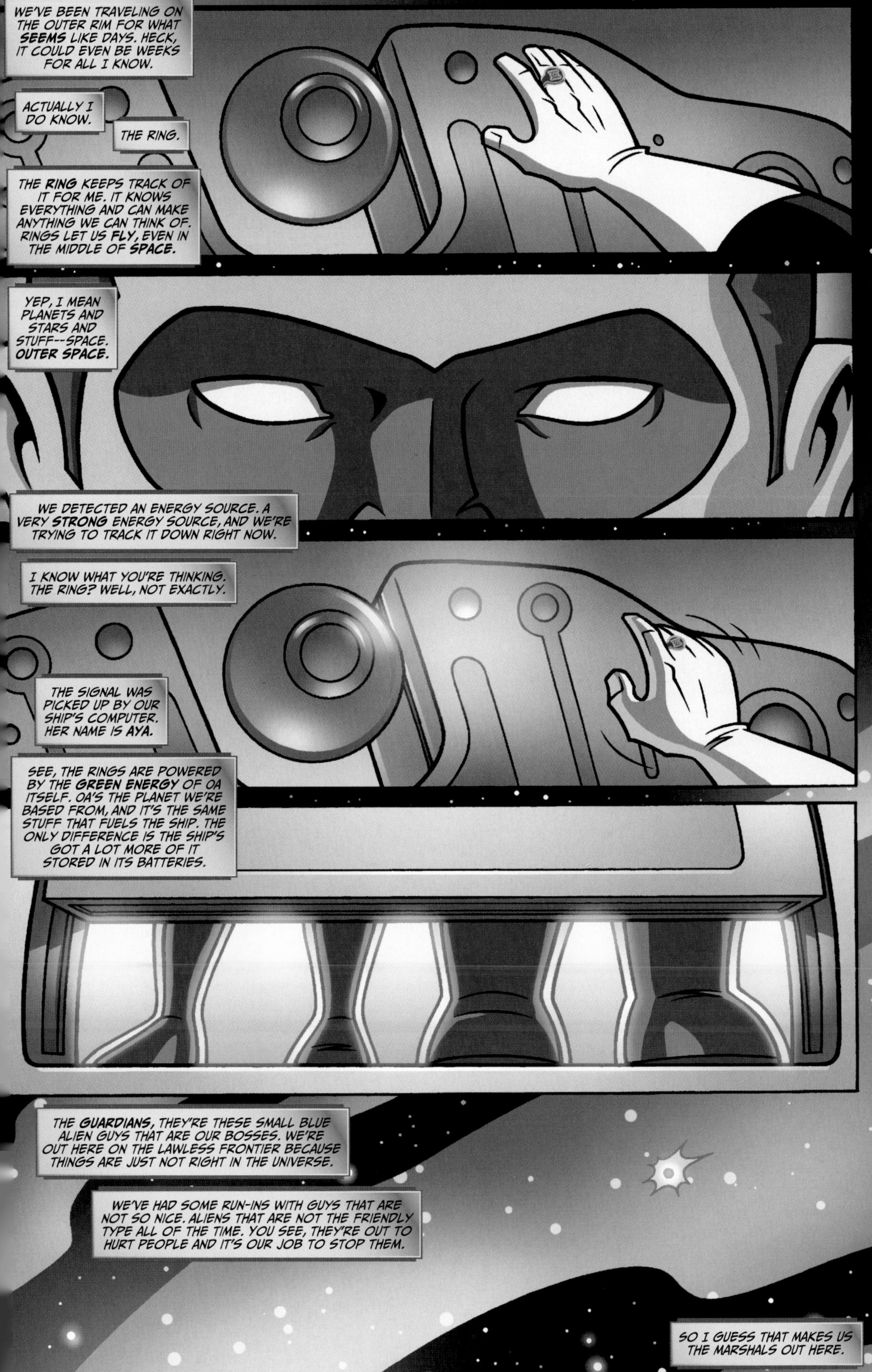
WE'VE BEEN TRAVELING ON THE OUTER RIM FOR WHAT SEEMS LIKE DAYS. HECK, IT COULD EVEN BE WEEKS FOR ALL I KNOW.
ACTUALLY I DO KNOW.
THE RING.
THE RING KEEPS TRACK OF IT FOR ME. IT KNOWS EVERYTHING AND CAN MAKE ANYTHING WE CAN THINK OF. RINGS LET US FLY, EVEN IN THE MIDDLE OF SPACE.
YEP, I MEAN PLANETS AND STARS AND STUFF--SPACE. OUTER SPACE.
WE DETECTED AN ENERGY SOURCE. A VERY STRONG ENERGY SOURCE, AND WE'RE TRYING TO TRACK IT DOWN RIGHT NOW.
I KNOW WHAT YOU'RE THINKING. THE RING? WELL, NOT EXACTLY.
THE SIGNAL WAS PICKED UP BY OUR SHIP'S COMPUTER. HER NAME IS AYA.
SEE, THE RINGS ARE POWERED BY THE GREEN ENERGY OF OA ITSELF. OA'S THE PLANET WE'RE BASED FROM, AND IT'S THE SAME STUFF THAT FUELS THE SHIP. THE ONLY DIFFERENCE IS THE SHIP'S GOT A LOT MORE OF IT STORED IN ITS BATTERIES.
THE GUARDIANS, THEY'RE THESE SMALL BLUE ALIEN GUYS THAT ARE OUR BOSSES. WE'RE OUT HERE ON THE LAWLESS FRONTIER BECAUSE THINGS ARE JUST NOT RIGHT IN THE UNIVERSE.
WE'VE HAD SOME RUN-INS WITH GUYS THAT ARE NOT SO NICE. ALIENS THAT ARE NOT THE FRIENDLY TYPE ALL OF THE TIME. YOU SEE, THEY'RE OUT TO HURT PEOPLE AND IT'S OUR JOB TO STOP THEM.
SO I GUESS THAT MAKES US THE MARSHALS OUT HERE.

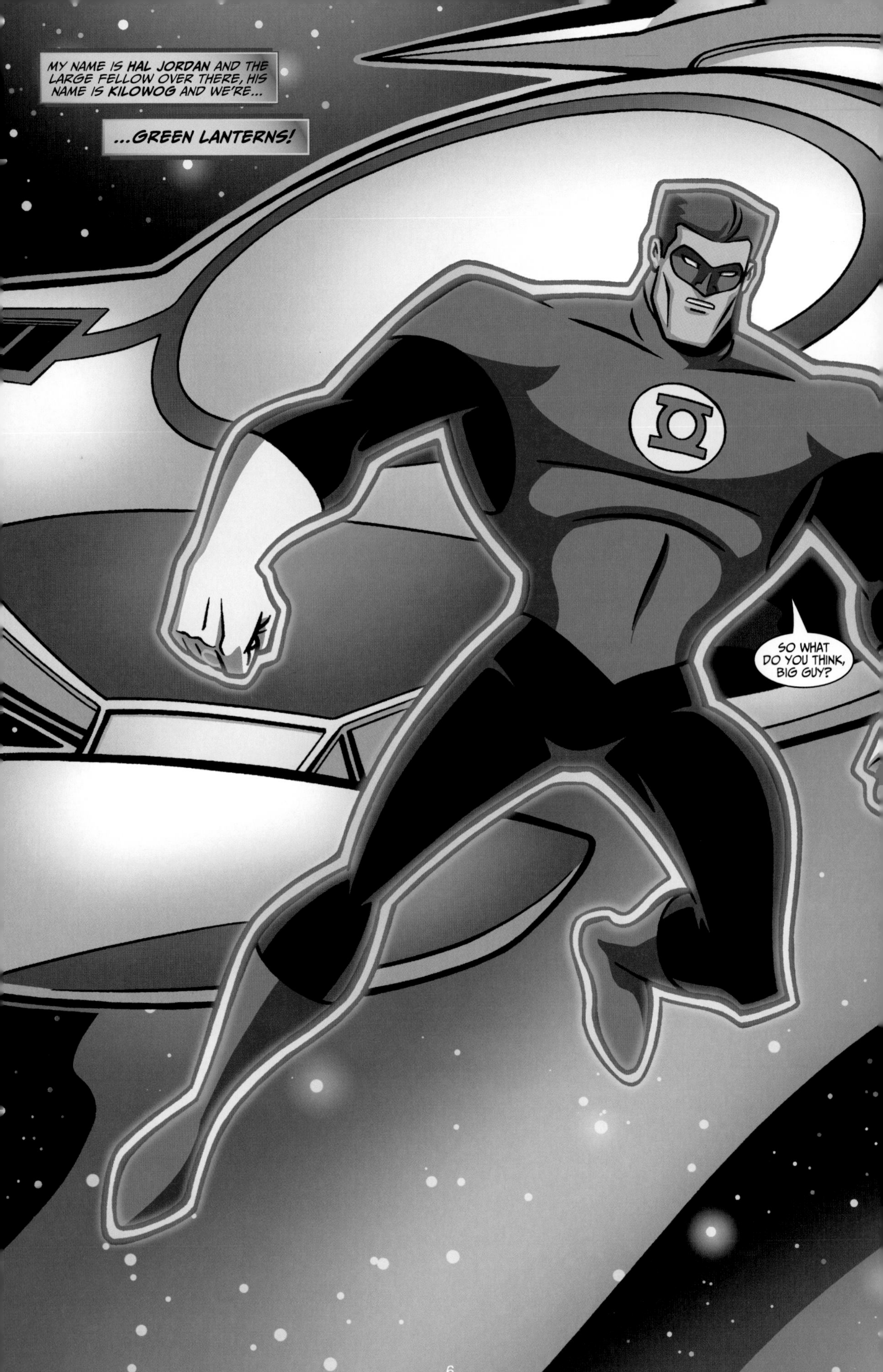
MY NAME IS HAL JORDAN AND THE LARGE FELLOW OVER THERE, HIS NAME IS KILOWOG AND WE'RE...
...GREEN LANTERNS!
SO WHAT DO YOU THINK, BIG GUY?

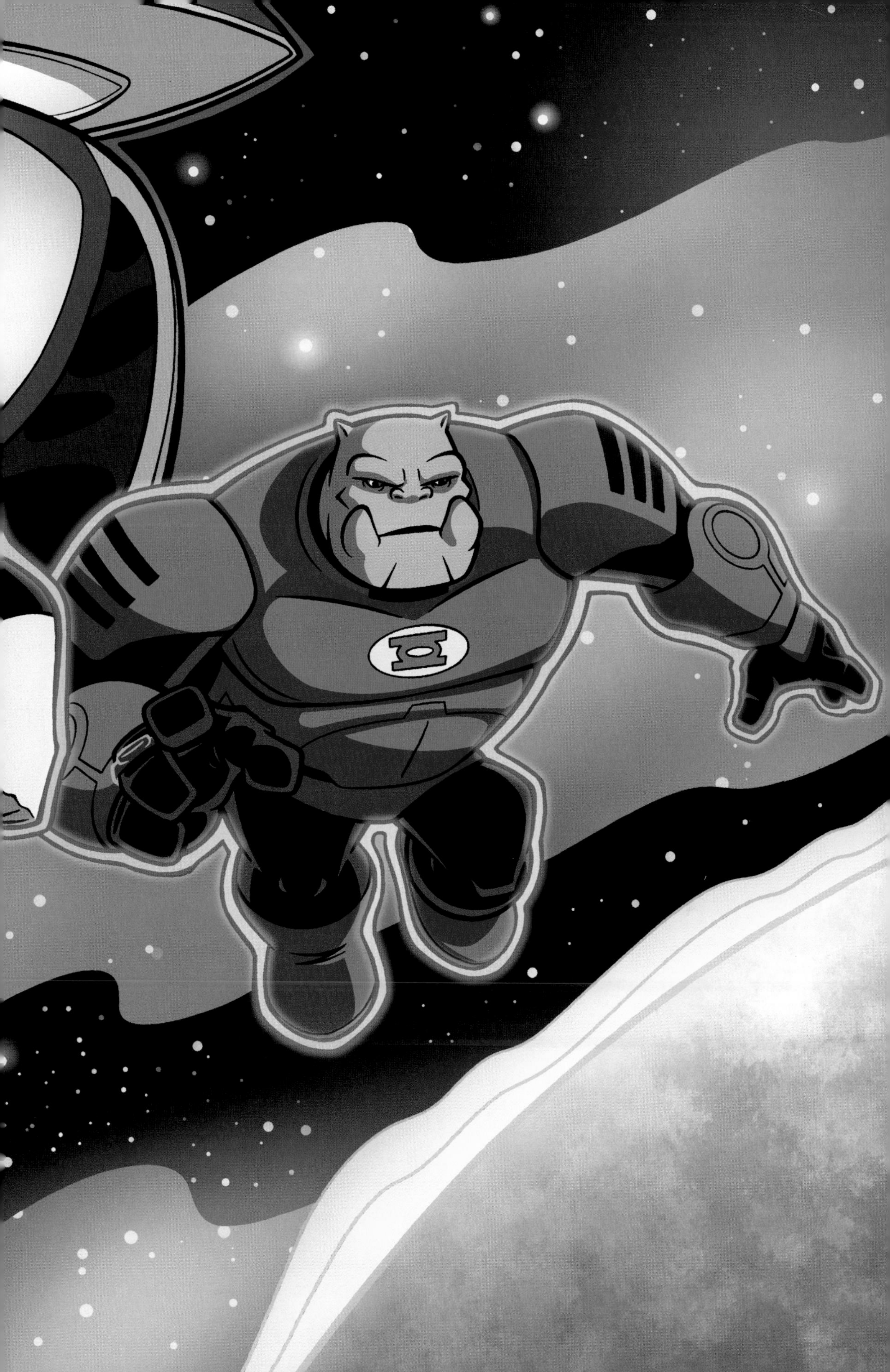

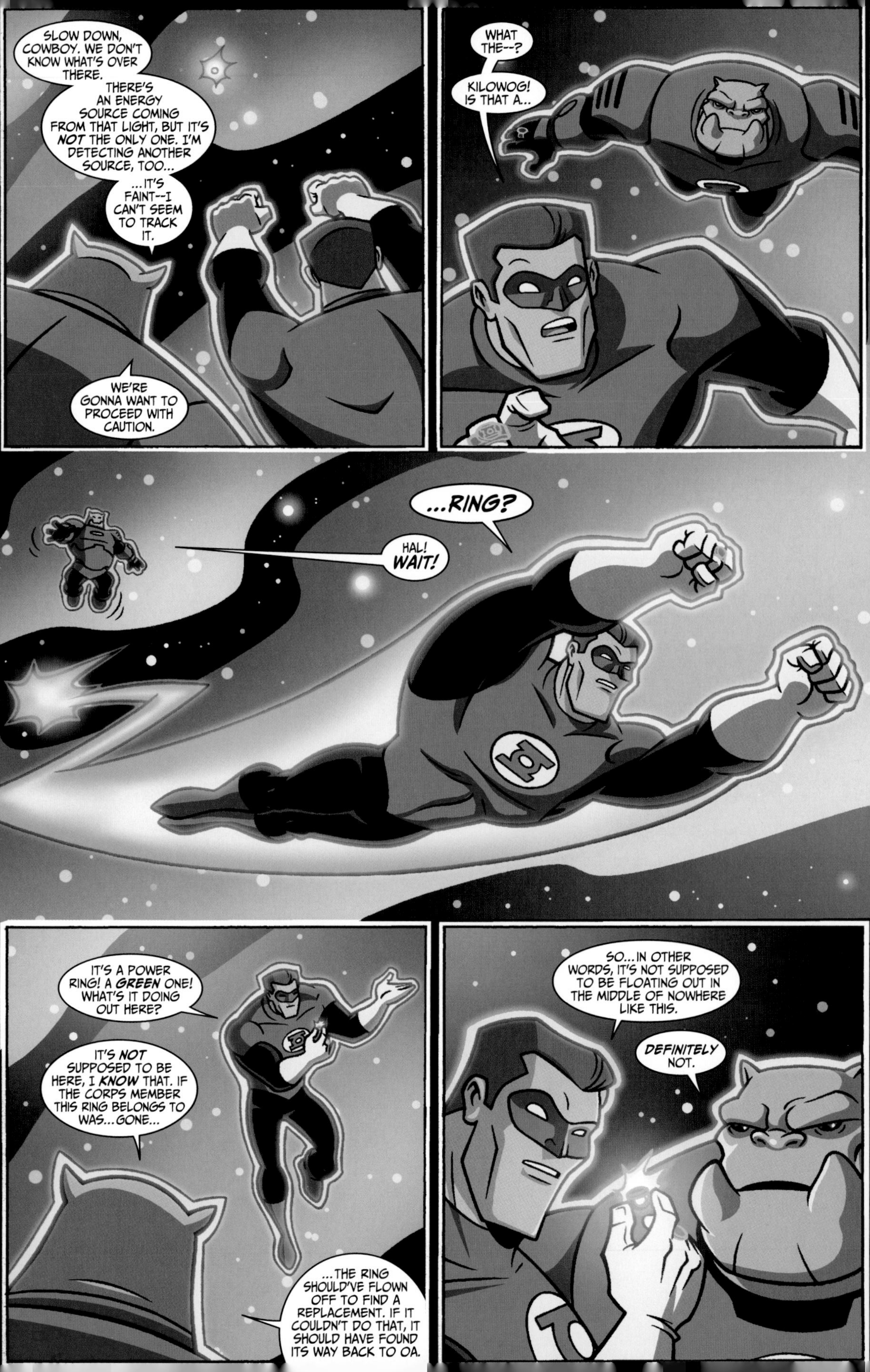
SLOW DOWN, COWBOY. WE DON'T KNOW WHAT'S OVER THERE.
THERE'S AN ENERGY SOURCE COMING FROM THAT LIGHT, BUT IT'S NOT THE ONLY ONE. I'M DETECTING ANOTHER SOURCE, TOO...
...IT'S FAINT--I CAN'T SEEM TO TRACK IT.
WE'RE GONNA WANT TO PROCEED WITH CAUTION.
WHAT THE--?
KILOWOG! IS THAT A...
...RING?
HAL! WAIT!
IT'S A POWER RING! A GREEN ONE! WHAT'S IT DOING OUT HERE?
IT'S NOT SUPPOSED TO BE HERE, I KNOW THAT. IF THE CORPS MEMBER THIS RING BELONGS TO WAS...GONE...
...THE RING SHOULD'VE FLOWN OFF TO FIND A REPLACEMENT. IF IT COULDN'T DO THAT, IT SHOULD HAVE FOUND ITS WAY BACK TO OA.
SO...IN OTHER WORDS, IT'S NOT SUPPOSED TO BE FLOATING OUT IN THE MIDDLE OF NOWHERE LIKE THIS.
DEFINITELY NOT.

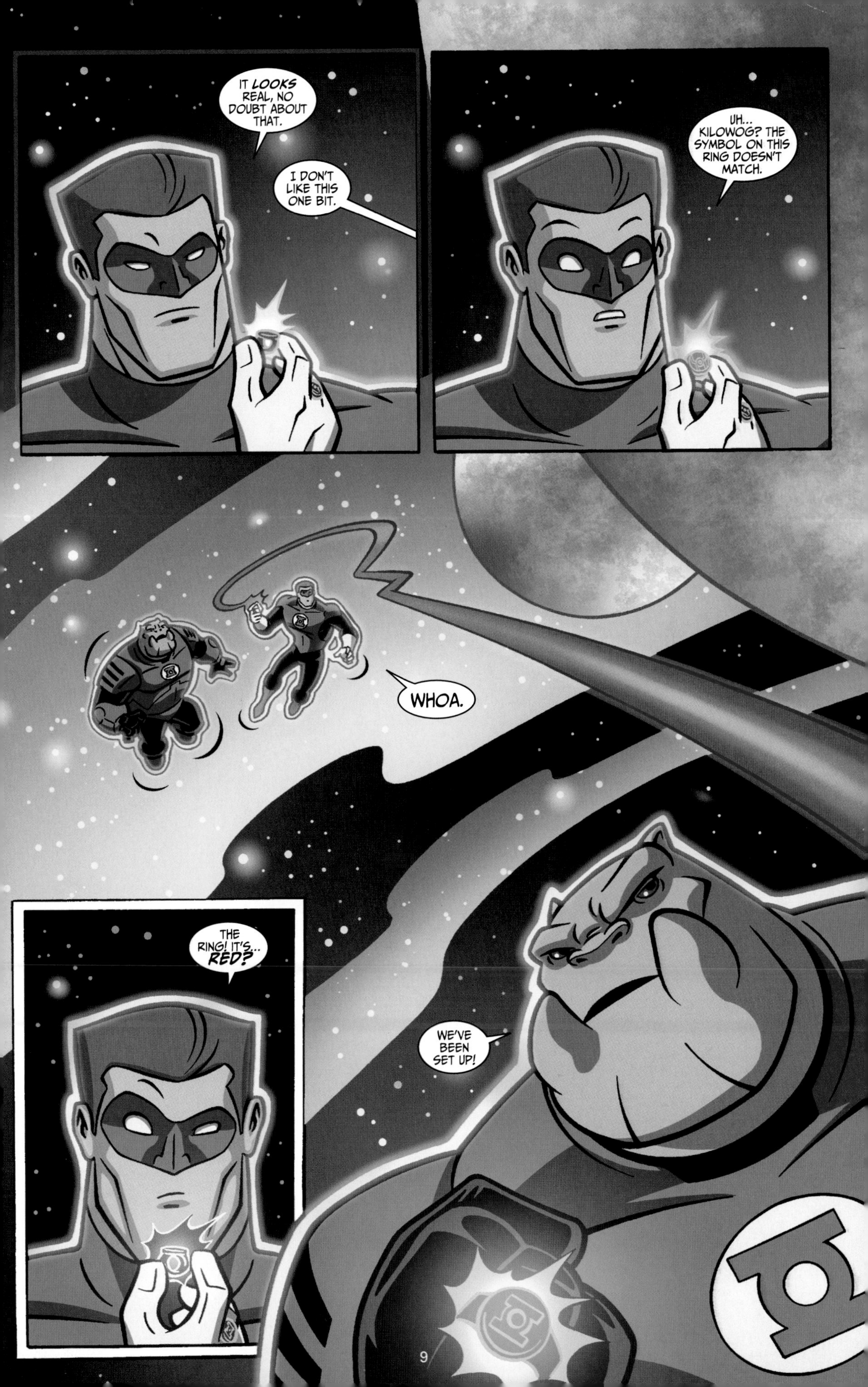
IT LOOKS REAL, NO DOUBT ABOUT THAT.
I DON'T LIKE THIS ONE BIT.
UH... KILOWOG? THE SYMBOL ON THIS RING DOESN'T MATCH.
WHOA.
THE RING! IT'S... RED?
WE'VE BEEN SET UP!

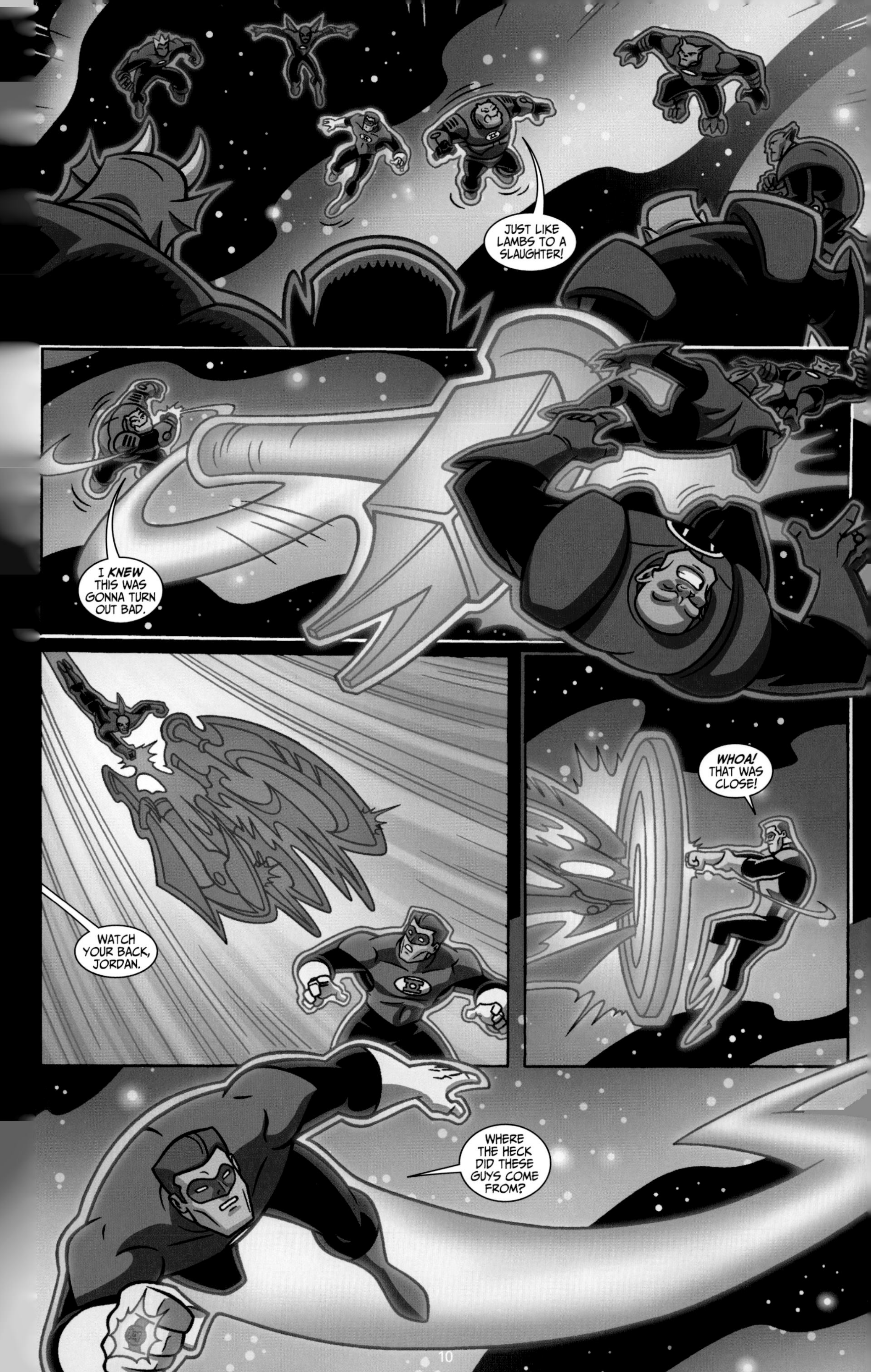
JUST LIKE LAMBS TO A SLAUGHTER!
I KNEW THIS WAS GONNA TURN OUT BAD.
WATCH YOUR BACK, JORDAN.
WHOA! THAT WAS CLOSE!
WHERE THE HECK DID THESE GUYS COME FROM?

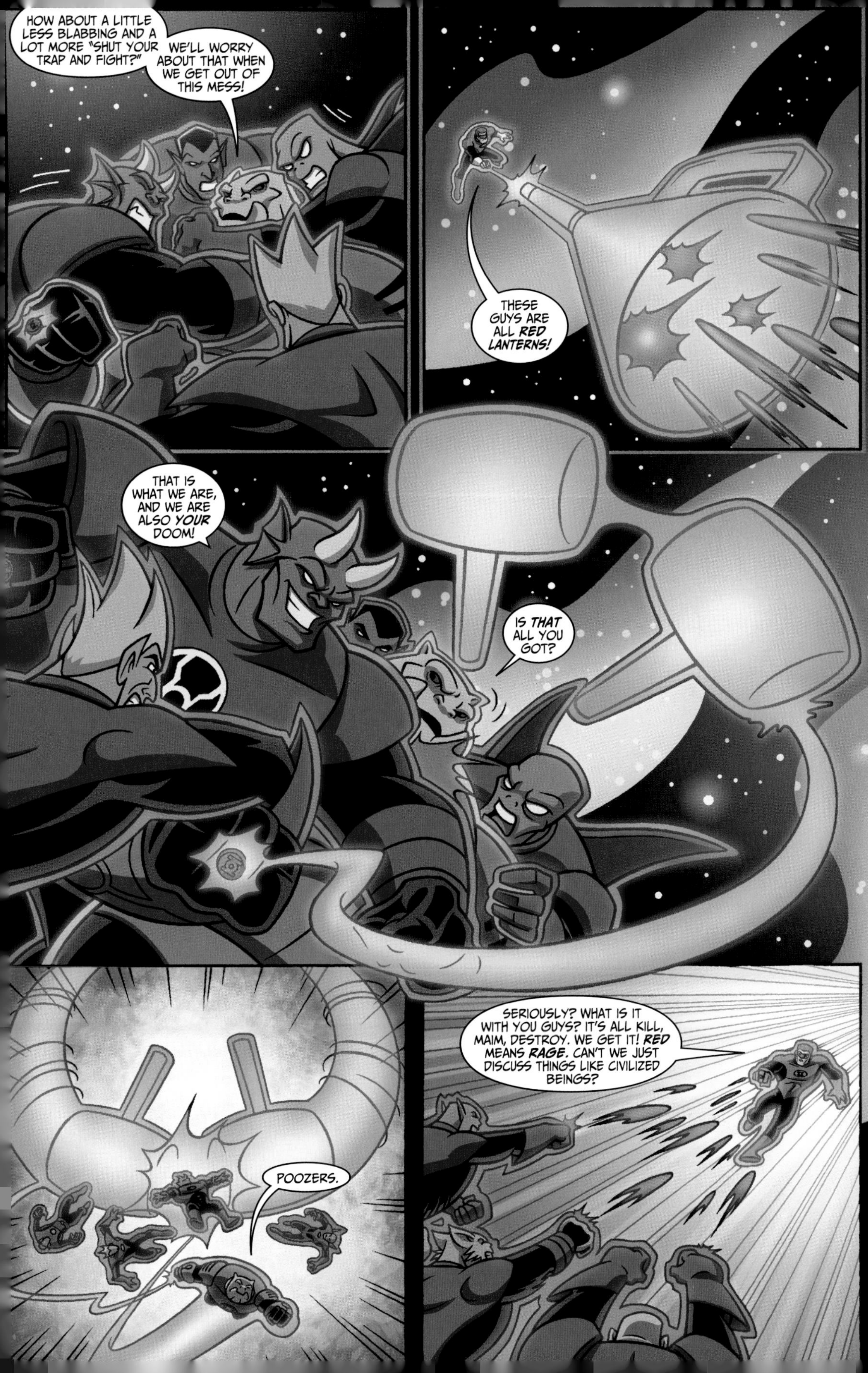
HOW ABOUT A LITTLE LESS BLABBING AND A LOT MORE "SHUT YOUR TRAP AND FIGHT?"
WE'LL WORRY ABOUT THAT WHEN WE GET OUT OF THIS MESS!
THESE GUYS ARE ALL RED LANTERNS!
THAT IS WHAT WE ARE, AND WE ARE ALSO YOUR DOOM!
IS THAT ALL YOU GOT?
POOZERS.
SERIOUSLY? WHAT IS IT WITH YOU GUYS? IT'S ALL KILL, MAIM, DESTROY. WE GET IT! RED MEANS RAGE. CAN'T WE JUST DISCUSS THINGS LIKE CIVILIZED BEINGS?

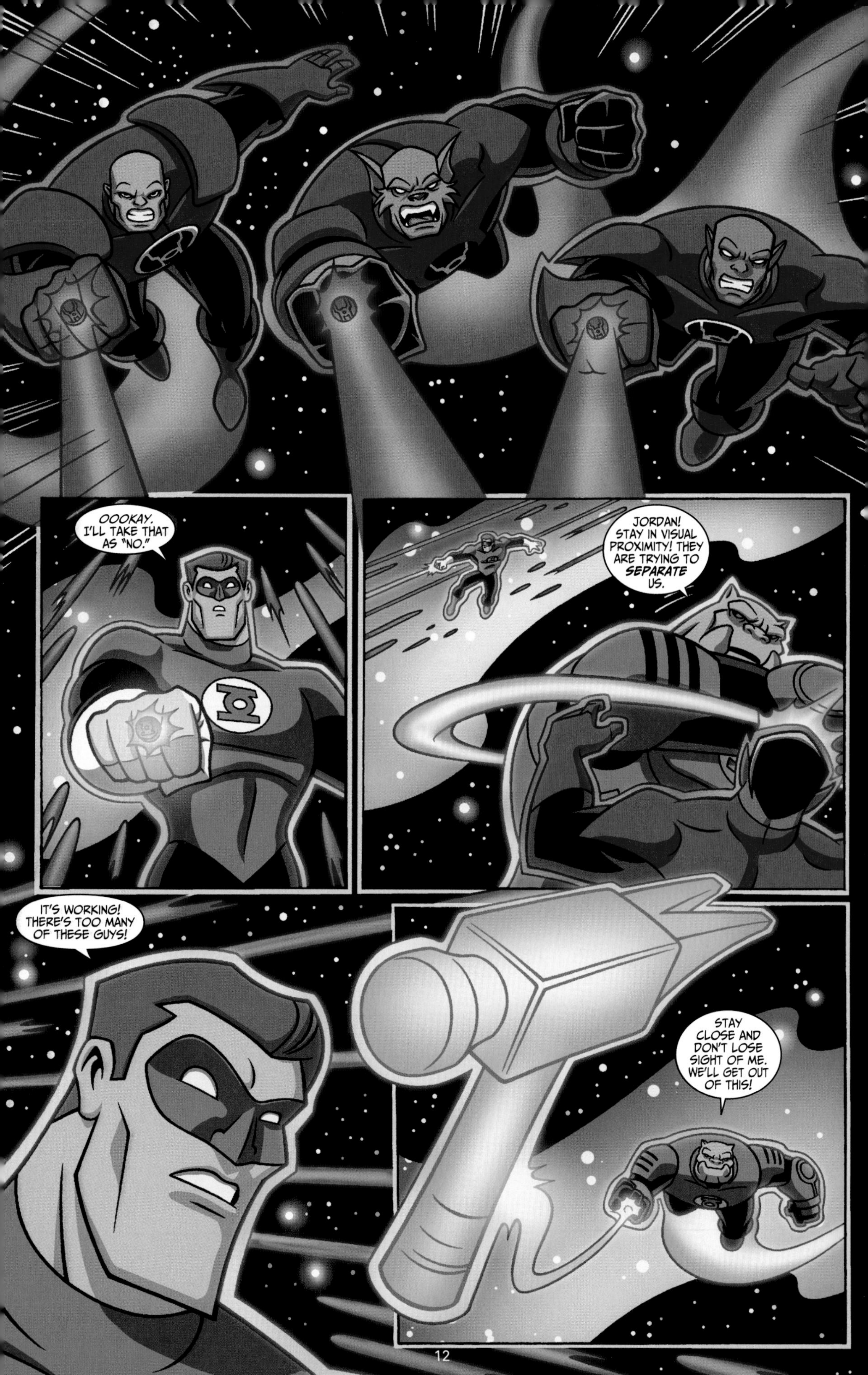
OOOKAY. I'LL TAKE THAT AS "NO."
JORDAN! STAY IN VISUAL PROXIMITY! THEY ARE TRYING TO SEPARATE US.
IT'S WORKING! THERE'S TOO MANY OF THESE GUYS!
STAY CLOSE AND DON'T LOSE SIGHT OF ME. WE'LL GET OUT OF THIS!

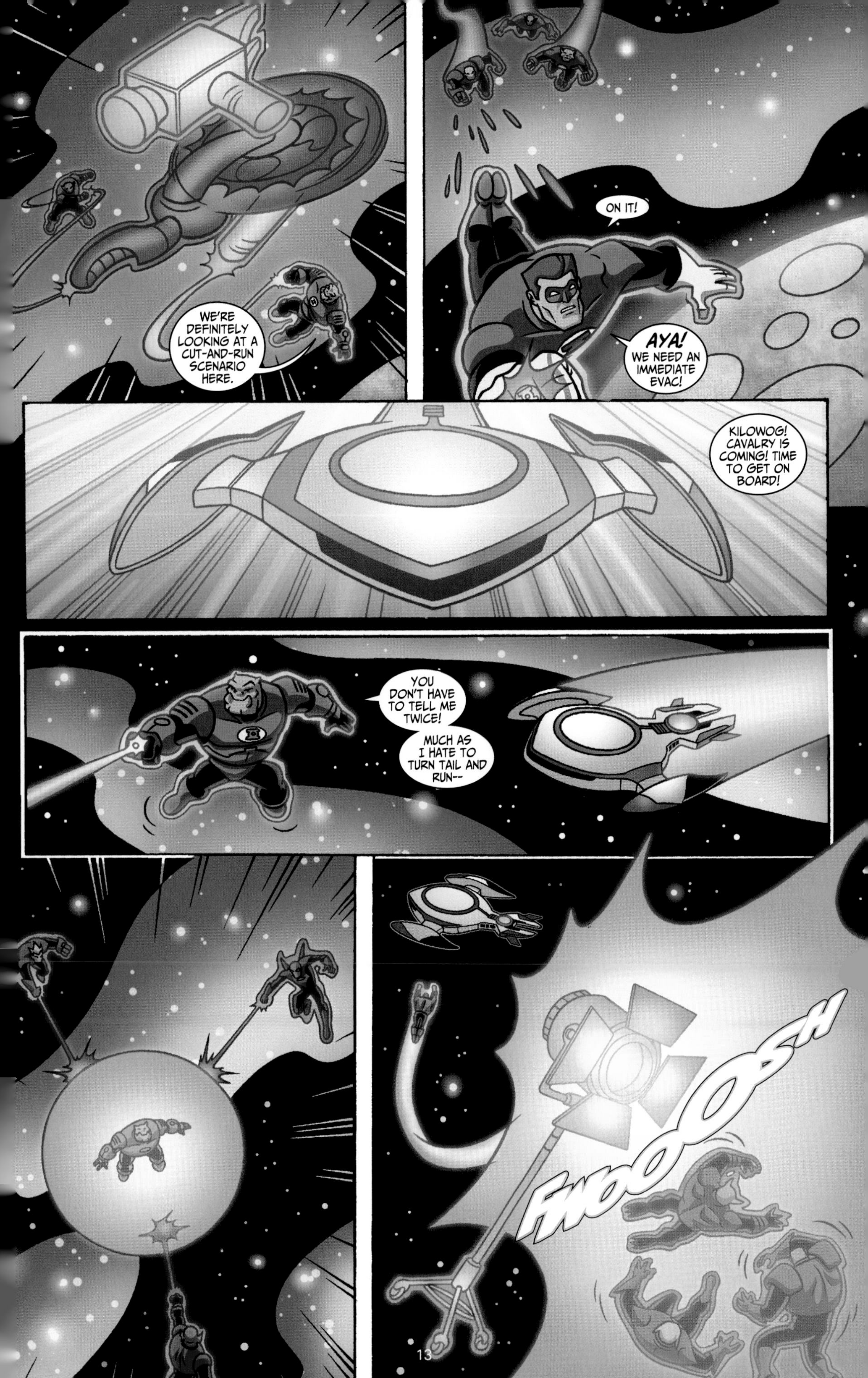
WE'RE DEFINITELY LOOKING AT A CUT-AND-RUN SCENARIO HERE.
ON IT!
AYA! WE NEED AN IMMEDIATE EVAC!
KILOWOG! CAVALRY IS COMING! TIME TO GET ON BOARD!
YOU DON'T HAVE TO TELL ME TWICE!
MUCH AS I HATE TO TURN TAIL AND RUN--
FWOOOOSH

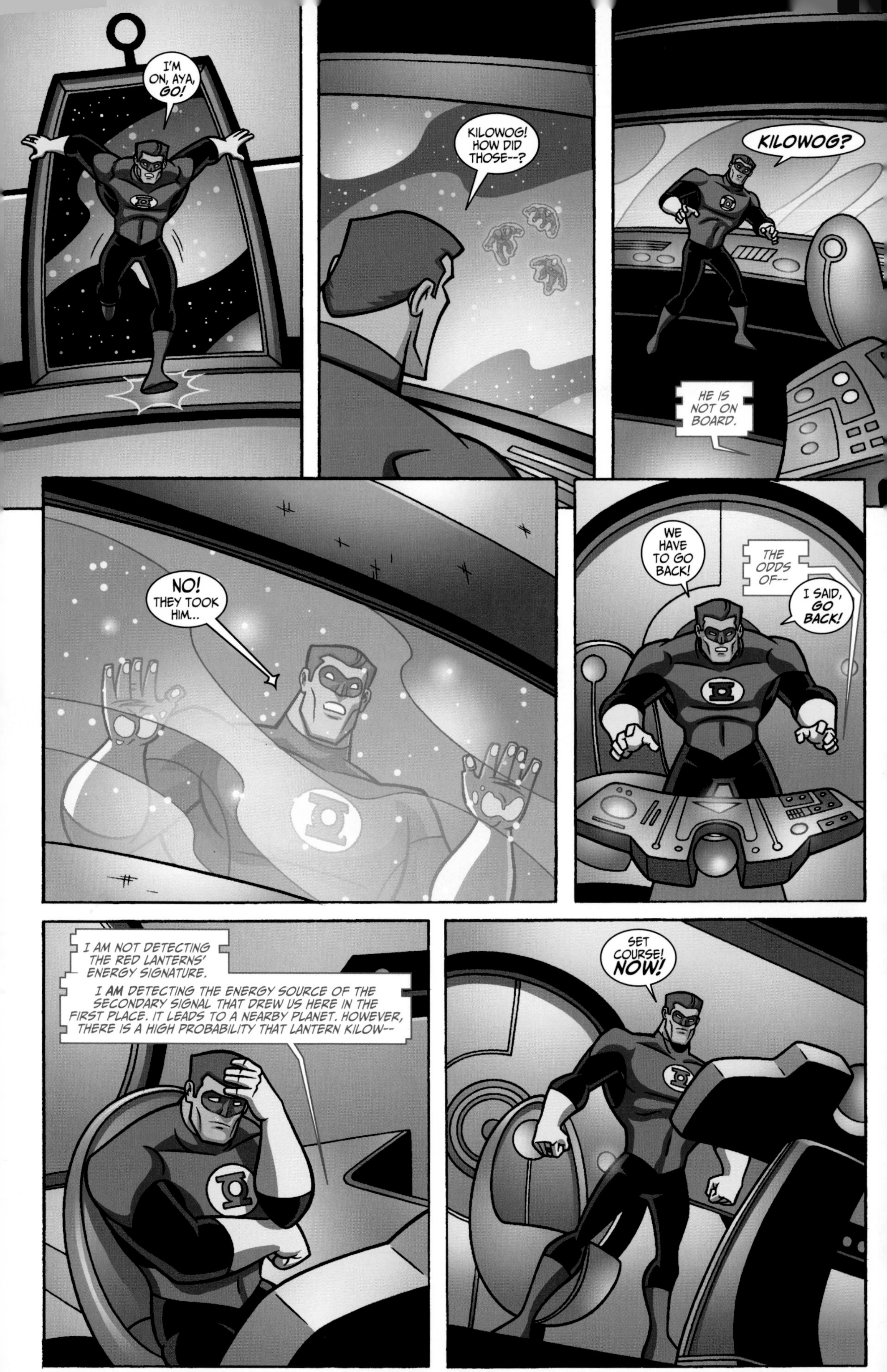
I'M ON, AYA, GO!
KILOWOG! HOW DID THOSE--?
KILOWOG?
HE IS NOT ON BOARD.
NO! THEY TOOK HIM...
WE HAVE TO GO BACK!
THE ODDS OF--
I SAID, GO BACK!
I AM NOT DETECTING THE RED LANTERNS' ENERGY SIGNATURE.
I AM DETECTING THE ENERGY SOURCE OF THE SECONDARY SIGNAL THAT DREW US HERE IN THE FIRST PLACE. IT LEADS TO A NEARBY PLANET. HOWEVER, THERE IS A HIGH PROBABILITY THAT LANTERN KILOW--
SET COURSE! NOW!

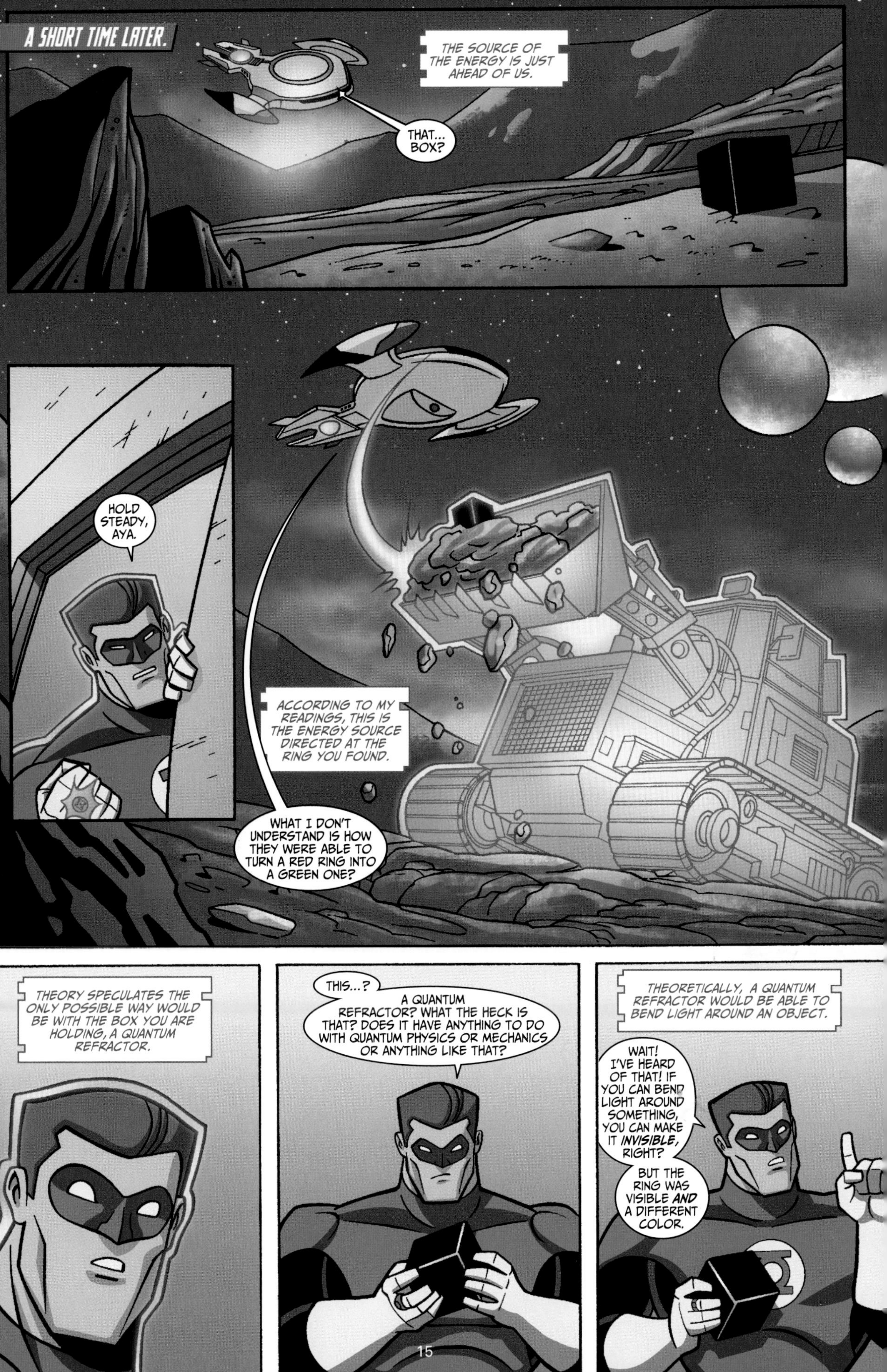
A SHORT TIME LATER.
THE SOURCE OF THE ENERGY IS JUST AHEAD OF US.
THAT... BOX?
HOLD STEADY, AYA.
ACCORDING TO MY READINGS, THIS IS THE ENERGY SOURCE DIRECTED AT THE RING YOU FOUND.
WHAT I DON'T UNDERSTAND IS HOW THEY WERE ABLE TO TURN A RED RING INTO A GREEN ONE?
THEORY SPECULATES THE ONLY POSSIBLE WAY WOULD BE WITH THE BOX YOU ARE HOLDING, A QUANTUM REFRACTOR.
THIS...?
A QUANTUM REFRACTOR? WHAT THE HECK IS THAT? DOES IT HAVE ANYTHING TO DO WITH QUANTUM PHYSICS OR MECHANICS OR ANYTHING LIKE THAT?
THEORETICALLY, A QUANTUM REFRACTOR WOULD BE ABLE TO BEND LIGHT AROUND AN OBJECT.
WAIT! I'VE HEARD OF THAT! IF YOU CAN BEND LIGHT AROUND SOMETHING, YOU CAN MAKE IT INVISIBLE, RIGHT?
BUT THE RING WAS VISIBLE AND A DIFFERENT COLOR.

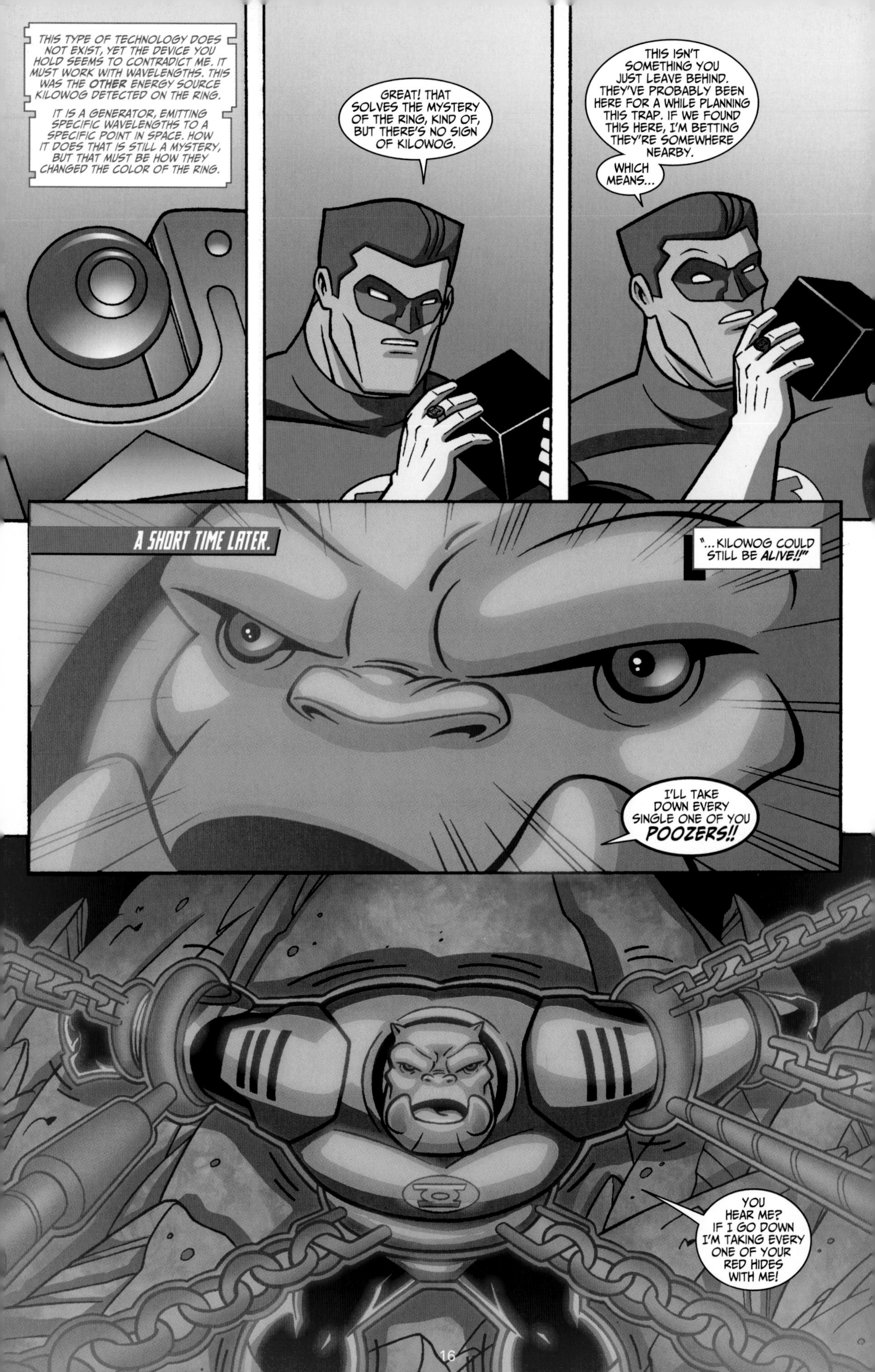
THIS TYPE OF TECHNOLOGY DOES NOT EXIST, YET THE DEVICE YOU HOLD SEEMS TO CONTRADICT ME. IT MUST WORK WITH WAVELENGTHS. THIS WAS THE OTHER ENERGY SOURCE KILOWOG DETECTED ON THE RING.
IT IS A GENERATOR, EMITTING SPECIFIC WAVELENGTHS TO A SPECIFIC POINT IN SPACE. HOW IT DOES THAT IS STILL A MYSTERY, BUT THAT MUST BE HOW THEY CHANGED THE COLOR OF THE RING.
GREAT! THAT SOLVES THE MYSTERY OF THE RING, KIND OF, BUT THERE'S NO SIGN OF KILOWOG.
THIS ISN'T SOMETHING YOU JUST LEAVE BEHIND. THEY'VE PROBABLY BEEN HERE FOR A WHILE PLANNING THIS TRAP. IF WE FOUND THIS HERE, I'M BETTING THEY'RE SOMEWHERE NEARBY.
WHICH MEANS...
A SHORT TIME LATER.
"...KILOWOG COULD STILL BE ALIVE!!"
I'LL TAKE DOWN EVERY SINGLE ONE OF YOU POOZERS!!
YOU HEAR ME? IF I GO DOWN I'M TAKING EVERY ONE OF YOUR RED HIDES WITH ME!

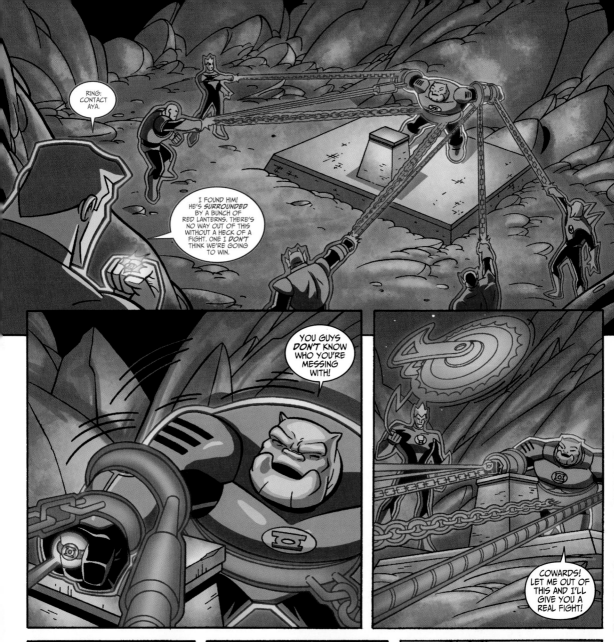

RING: CONTACT AYA.

I FOUND HIM! HE'S *SURROUNDED* BY A BUNCH OF RED LANTERNS. THERE'S NO WAY OUT OF THIS WITHOUT A HECK OF A FIGHT. ONE I *DON'T* THINK WE'RE GOING TO WIN.

YOU GUYS *DON'T* KNOW WHO YOU'RE MESSING WITH!

COWARDS! LET ME OUT OF THIS AND I'LL GIVE YOU A *REAL* FIGHT!

THEY'RE GOING TO CUT OFF HIS ARM?! IF THEY KILL A GREEN LANTERN, THEIR RING FLIES OFF TO FIND A SUBSTITUTE...

...THEY TOOK HIM ALIVE TO TRY AND GET THE RING!

THEY NOT ONLY WANT TO GET RID OF US BUT THEY WANT... ...A GREEN RING. *A REAL ONE!*

WE'VE GOT TO DO SOMETHING!

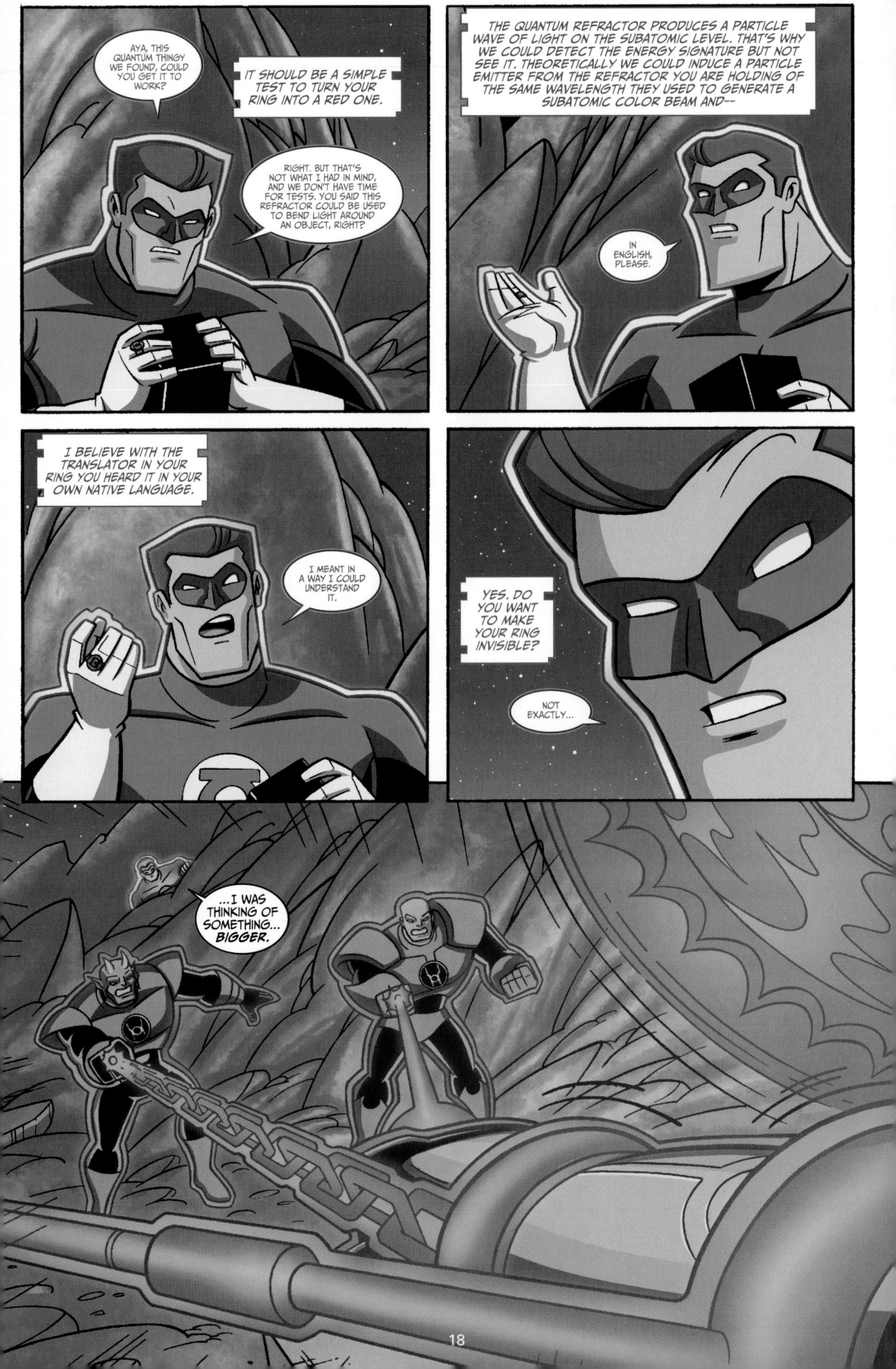
AYA, THIS QUANTUM THINGY WE FOUND, COULD YOU GET IT TO WORK?
IT SHOULD BE A SIMPLE TEST TO TURN YOUR RING INTO A RED ONE.
RIGHT. BUT THAT'S NOT WHAT I HAD IN MIND, AND WE DON'T HAVE TIME FOR TESTS. YOU SAID THIS REFRACTOR COULD BE USED TO BEND LIGHT AROUND AN OBJECT, RIGHT?
THE QUANTUM REFRACTOR PRODUCES A PARTICLE WAVE OF LIGHT ON THE SUBATOMIC LEVEL. THAT'S WHY WE COULD DETECT THE ENERGY SIGNATURE BUT NOT SEE IT. THEORETICALLY WE COULD INDUCE A PARTICLE EMITTER FROM THE REFRACTOR YOU ARE HOLDING OF THE SAME WAVELENGTH THEY USED TO GENERATE A SUBATOMIC COLOR BEAM AND--
IN ENGLISH, PLEASE.
I BELIEVE WITH THE TRANSLATOR IN YOUR RING YOU HEARD IT IN YOUR OWN NATIVE LANGUAGE.
I MEANT IN A WAY I COULD UNDERSTAND IT.
YES. DO YOU WANT TO MAKE YOUR RING INVISIBLE?
NOT EXACTLY...
...I WAS THINKING OF SOMETHING... BIGGER.

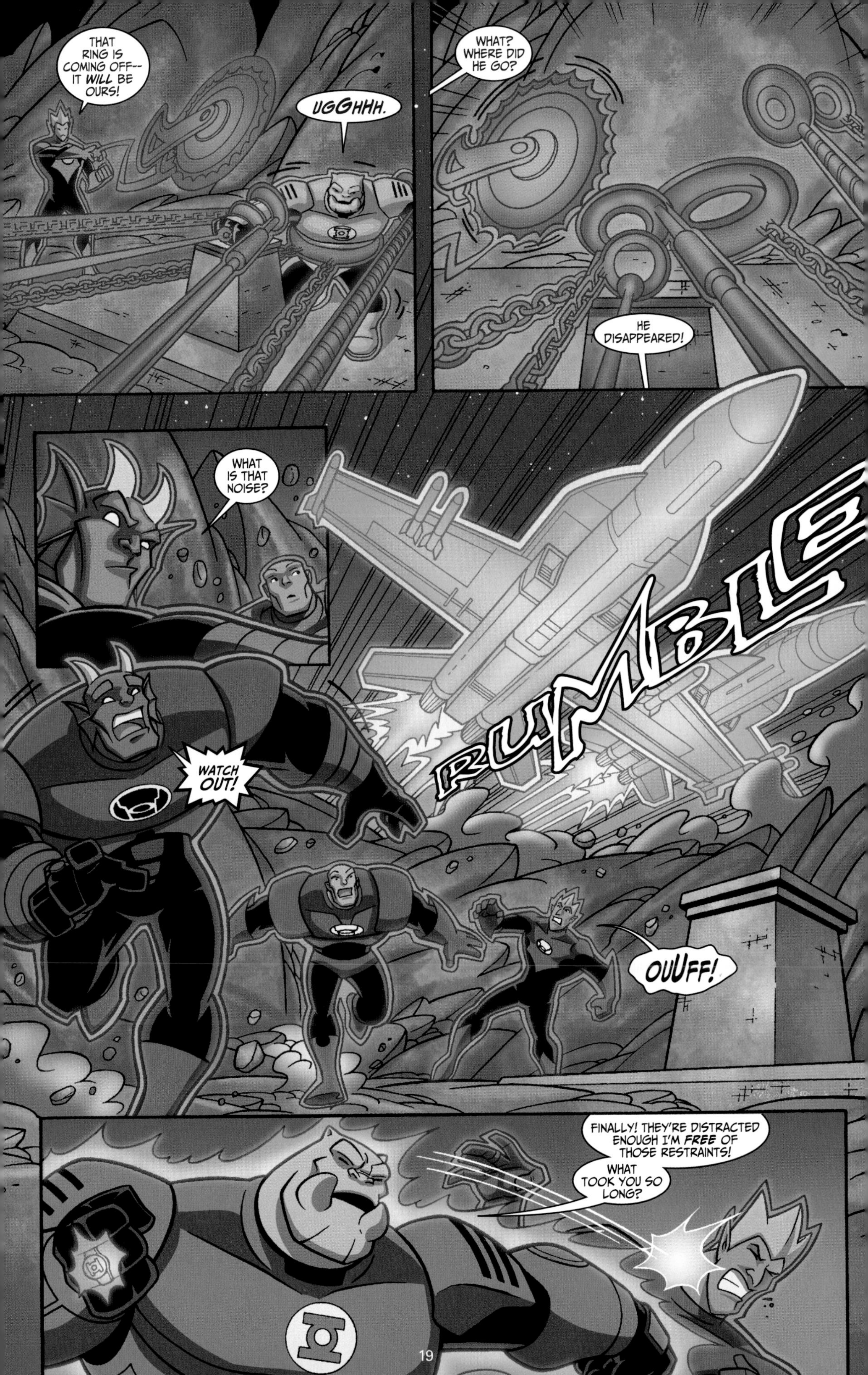

THAT RING IS COMING OFF-- IT WILL BE OURS!
UGGHHH.
WHAT? WHERE DID HE GO?
HE DISAPPEARED!
WHAT IS THAT NOISE?
RUMBLE
WATCH OUT!
OUUFF!
FINALLY! THEY'RE DISTRACTED ENOUGH I'M FREE OF THOSE RESTRAINTS!
WHAT TOOK YOU SO LONG?

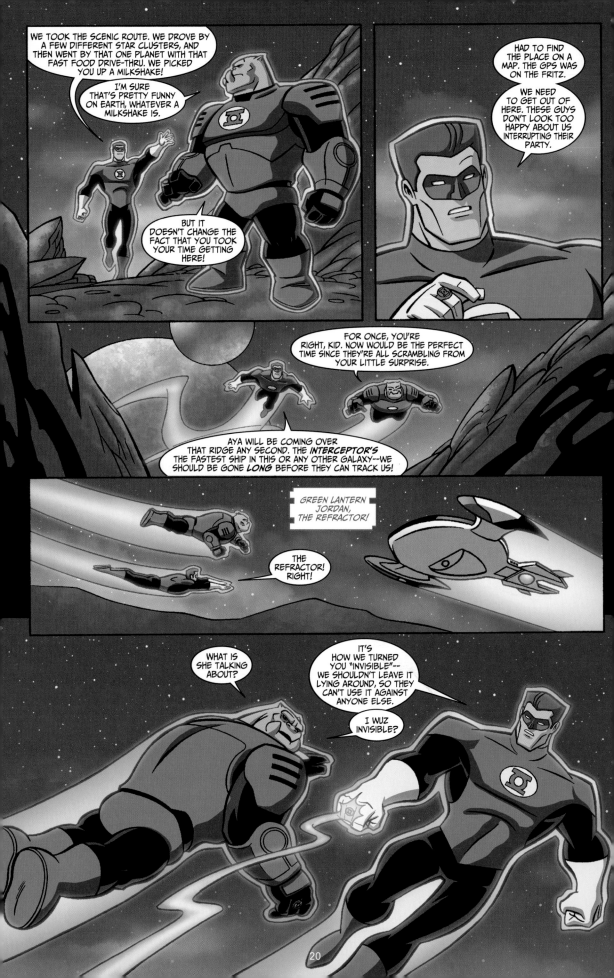

WE TOOK THE SCENIC ROUTE. WE DROVE BY A FEW DIFFERENT STAR CLUSTERS, AND THEN WENT BY THAT ONE PLANET WITH THAT FAST FOOD DRIVE-THRU. WE PICKED YOU UP A MILKSHAKE!

I'M SURE THAT'S PRETTY FUNNY ON EARTH, WHATEVER A MILKSHAKE IS.

BUT IT DOESN'T CHANGE THE FACT THAT YOU TOOK YOUR TIME GETTING HERE!

HAD TO FIND THE PLACE ON A MAP. THE GPS WAS ON THE FRITZ.

WE NEED TO GET OUT OF HERE. THESE GUYS DON'T LOOK TOO HAPPY ABOUT US INTERRUPTING THEIR PARTY.

FOR ONCE, YOU'RE RIGHT, KID. NOW WOULD BE THE PERFECT TIME SINCE THEY'RE ALL SCRAMBLING FROM YOUR LITTLE SURPRISE.

AYA WILL BE COMING OVER THAT RIDGE ANY SECOND. THE *INTERCEPTOR'S* THE FASTEST SHIP IN THIS OR ANY OTHER GALAXY--WE SHOULD BE GONE *LONG* BEFORE THEY CAN TRACK US!

GREEN LANTERN JORDAN, THE REFRACTOR!

THE REFRACTOR! RIGHT!

WHAT IS SHE TALKING ABOUT?

IT'S HOW WE TURNED YOU "INVISIBLE"-- WE SHOULDN'T LEAVE IT LYING AROUND, SO THEY CAN'T USE IT AGAINST ANYONE ELSE.

I WUZ INVISIBLE?

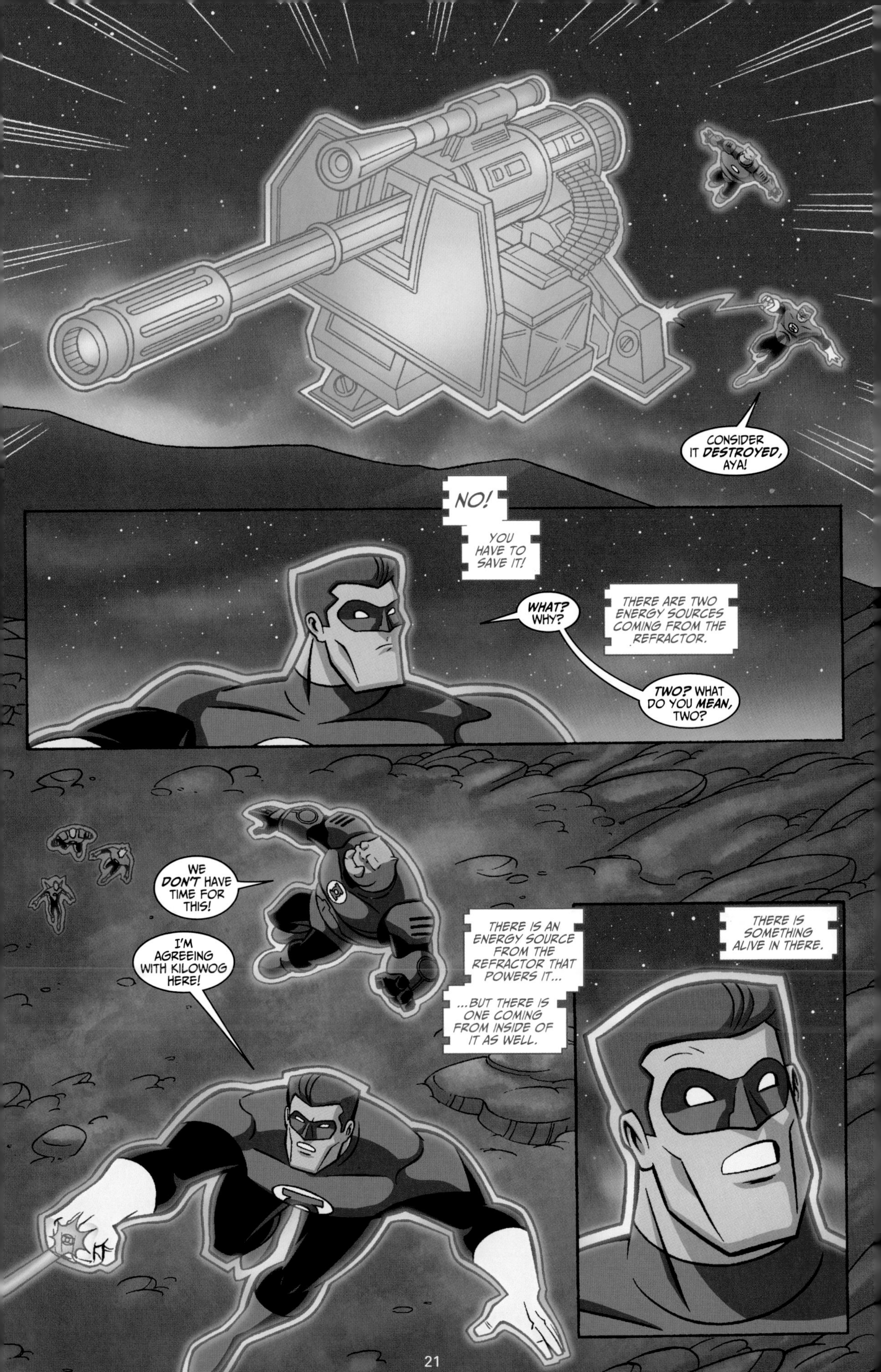
CONSIDER IT DESTROYED, AYA!
NO!
YOU HAVE TO SAVE IT!
WHAT? WHY?
THERE ARE TWO ENERGY SOURCES COMING FROM THE REFRACTOR.
TWO? WHAT DO YOU MEAN, TWO?
WE DON'T HAVE TIME FOR THIS!
I'M AGREEING WITH KILOWOG HERE!
THERE IS AN ENERGY SOURCE FROM THE REFRACTOR THAT POWERS IT...
...BUT THERE IS ONE COMING FROM INSIDE OF IT AS WELL.
THERE IS SOMETHING ALIVE IN THERE.

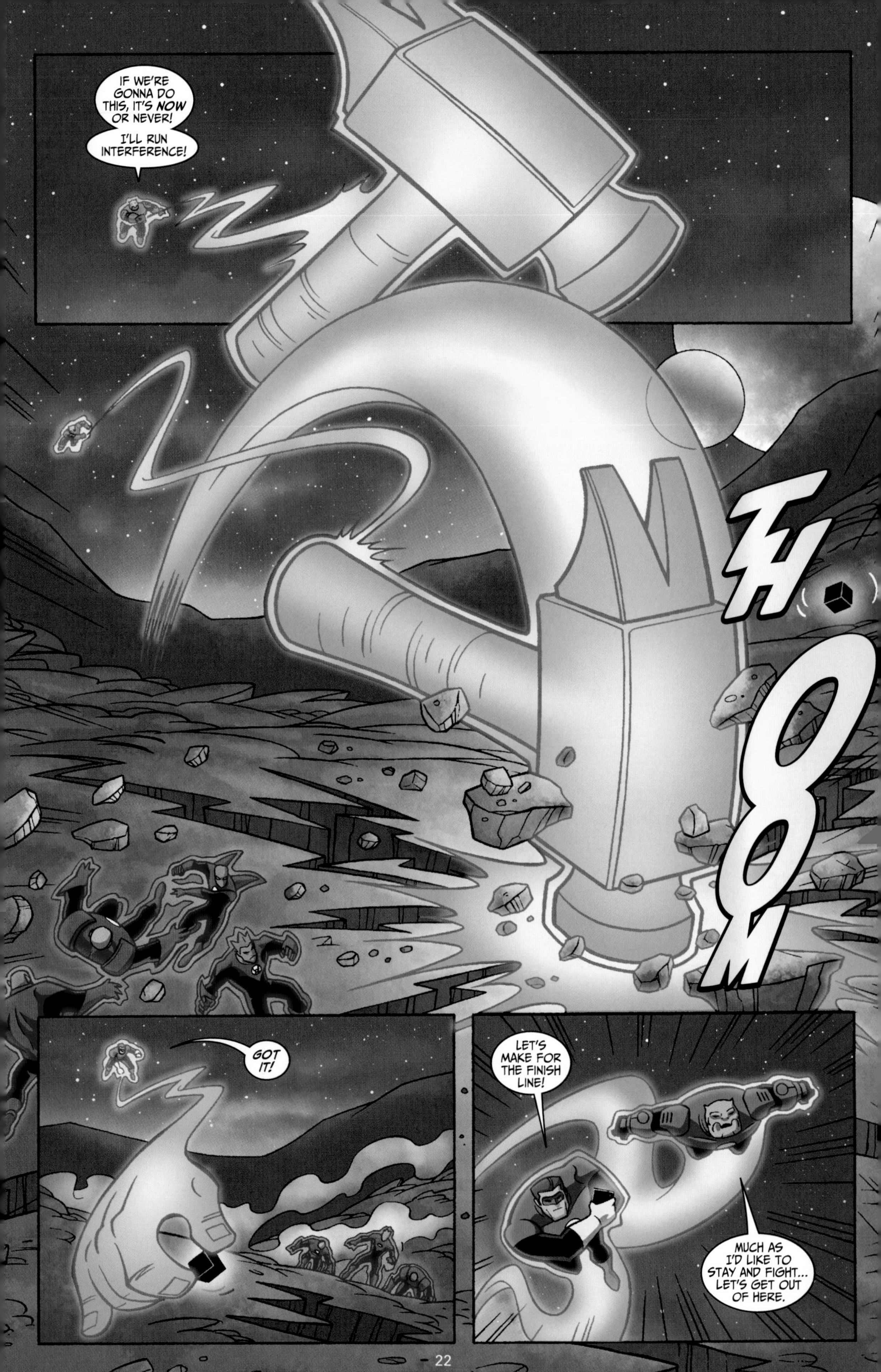
IF WE'RE GONNA DO THIS, IT'S *NOW* OR NEVER!
I'LL RUN INTERFERENCE!
THOOM
GOT IT!
LET'S MAKE FOR THE FINISH LINE!
MUCH AS I'D LIKE TO STAY AND FIGHT... LET'S GET OUT OF HERE.

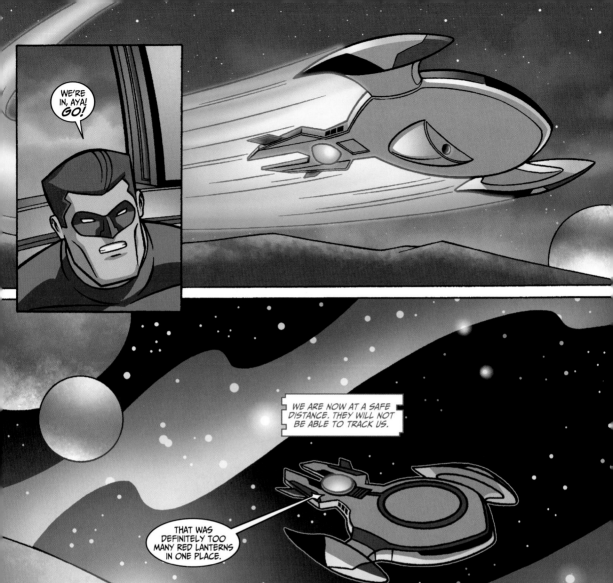

WE'RE IN, AYA! GO!

WE ARE NOW AT A SAFE DISTANCE. THEY WILL NOT BE ABLE TO TRACK US.

THAT WAS DEFINITELY TOO MANY RED LANTERNS IN ONE PLACE.

RIGHT NOW I'M WONDERING IF GOING BACK FOR THIS WAS WORTH IT.

LET'S TAKE A LOOK INSIDE, SHALL WE?

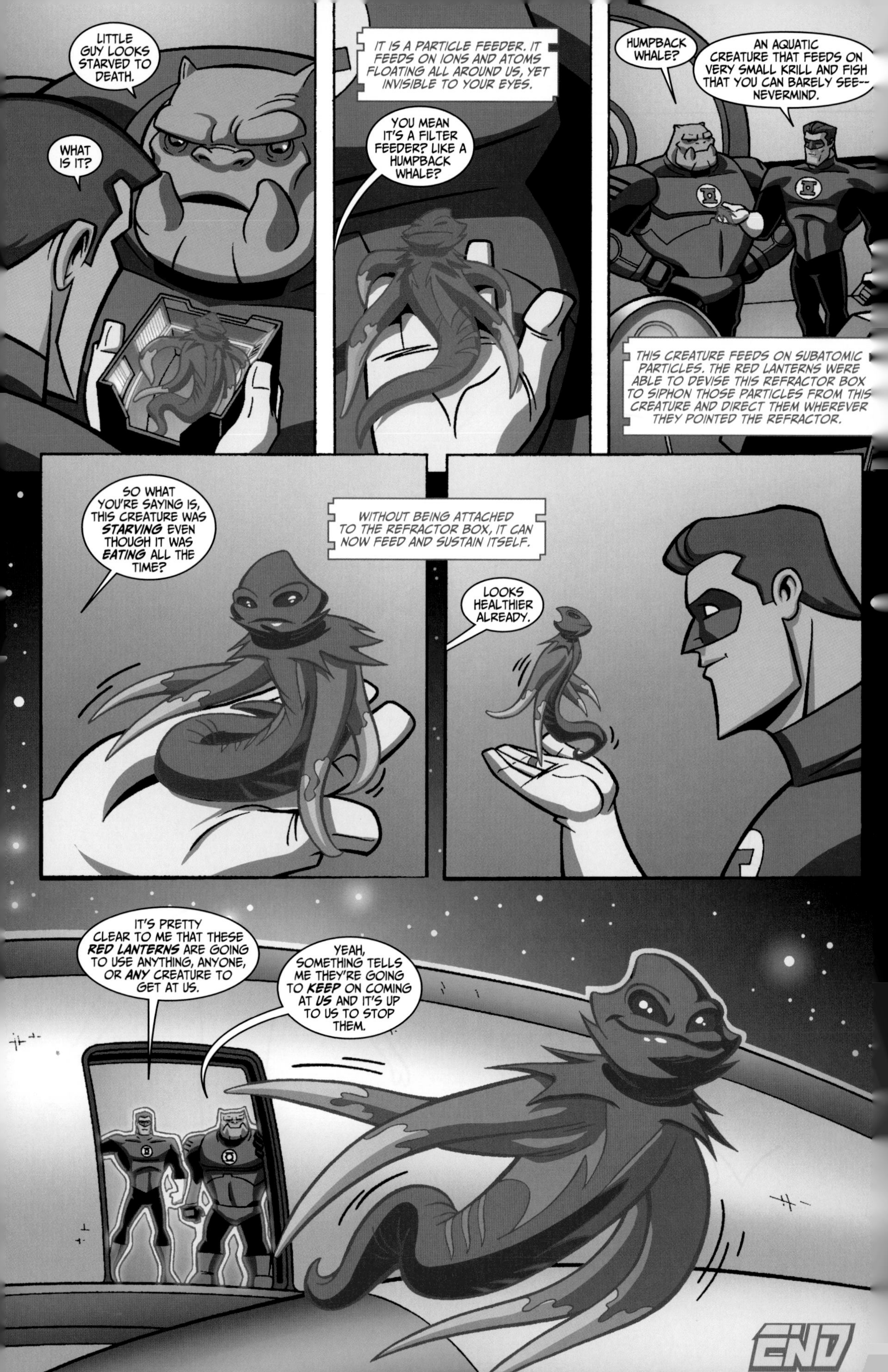
LITTLE GUY LOOKS STARVED TO DEATH.
WHAT IS IT?
IT IS A PARTICLE FEEDER. IT FEEDS ON IONS AND ATOMS FLOATING ALL AROUND US, YET INVISIBLE TO YOUR EYES.
YOU MEAN IT'S A FILTER FEEDER? LIKE A HUMPBACK WHALE?
HUMPBACK WHALE?
AN AQUATIC CREATURE THAT FEEDS ON VERY SMALL KRILL AND FISH THAT YOU CAN BARELY SEE-- NEVERMIND.
THIS CREATURE FEEDS ON SUBATOMIC PARTICLES. THE RED LANTERNS WERE ABLE TO DEVISE THIS REFRACTOR BOX TO SIPHON THOSE PARTICLES FROM THIS CREATURE AND DIRECT THEM WHEREVER THEY POINTED THE REFRACTOR.
SO WHAT YOU'RE SAYING IS, THIS CREATURE WAS STARVING EVEN THOUGH IT WAS EATING ALL THE TIME?
WITHOUT BEING ATTACHED TO THE REFRACTOR BOX, IT CAN NOW FEED AND SUSTAIN ITSELF.
LOOKS HEALTHIER ALREADY.
IT'S PRETTY CLEAR TO ME THAT THESE RED LANTERNS ARE GOING TO USE ANYTHING, ANYONE, OR ANY CREATURE TO GET AT US.
YEAH, SOMETHING TELLS ME THEY'RE GOING TO KEEP ON COMING AT US AND IT'S UP TO US TO STOP THEM.
END

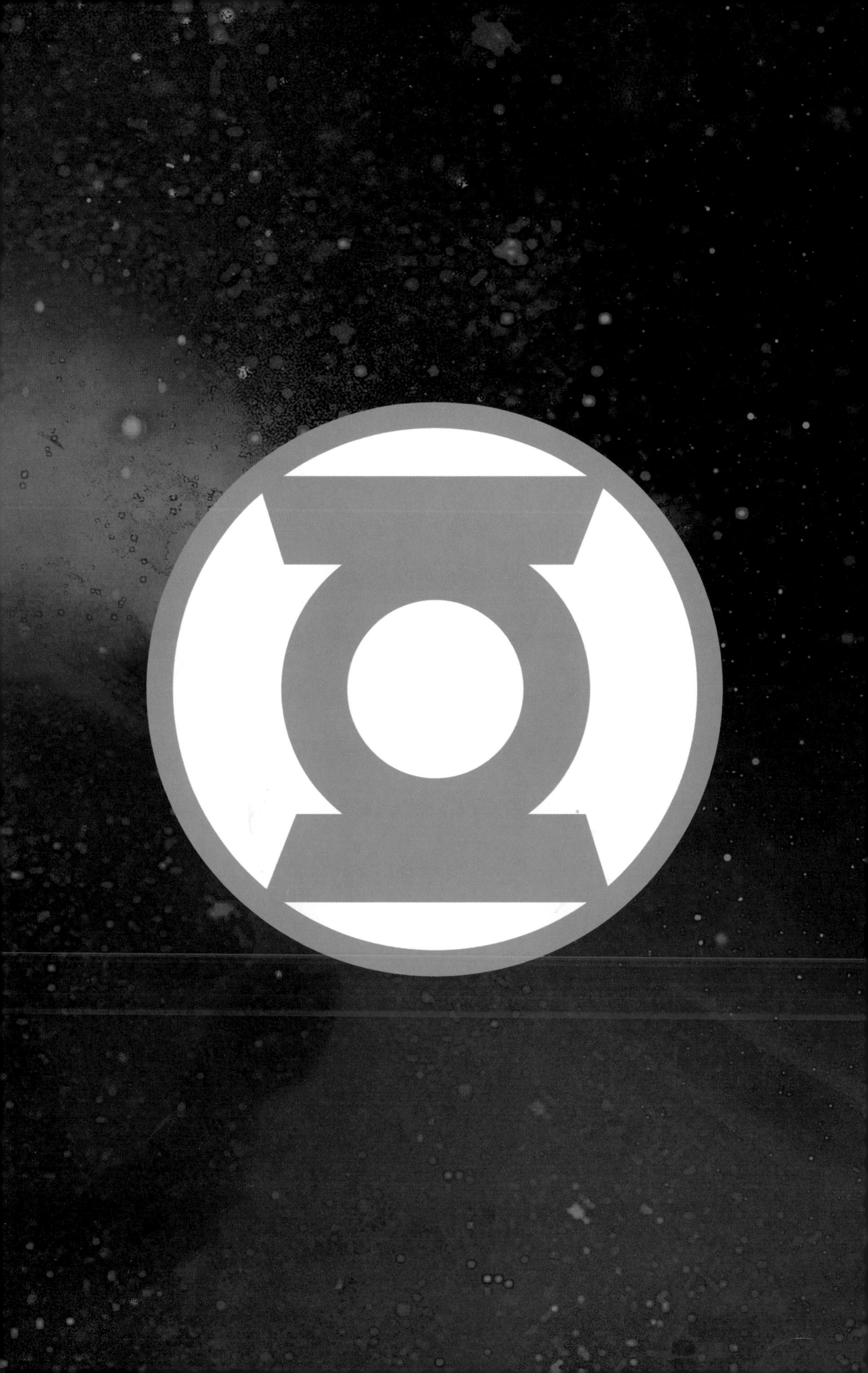

DRAW YOUR OWN HAL JORDAN, GREEN LANTERN!

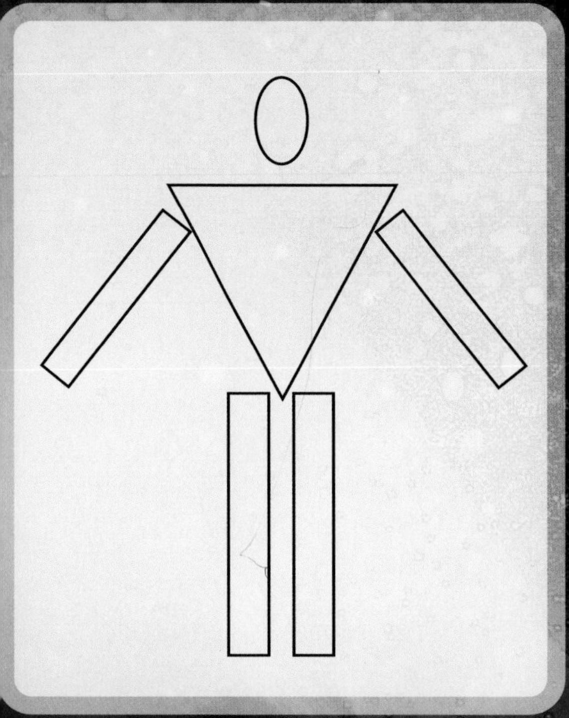

1.) Using a pencil, start with some basic shapes to build a "body."

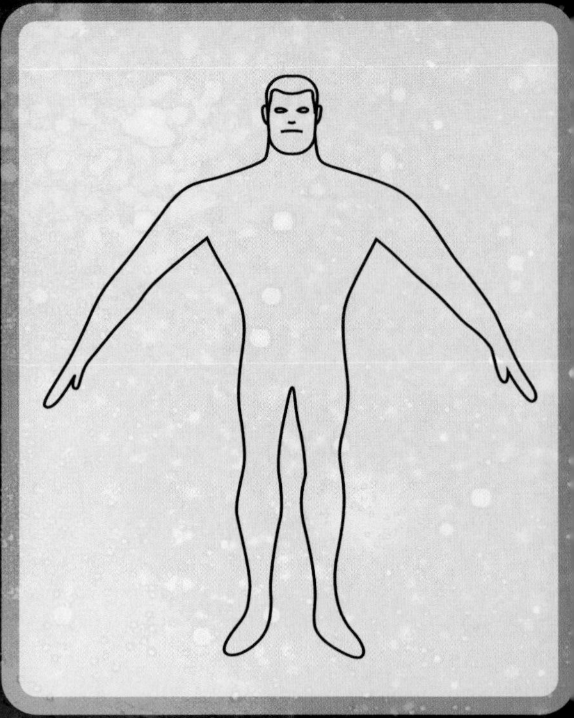

2.) Smooth your outline, and begin adding facial features.

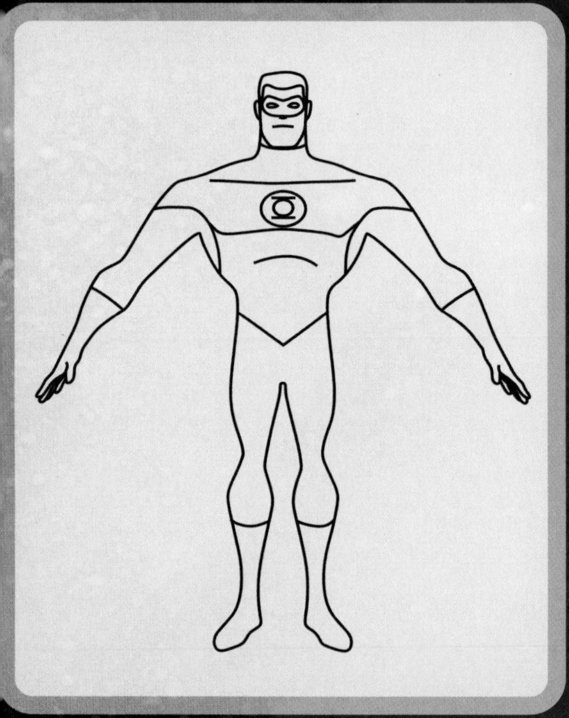

3.) Add in costume details, like Hal's mask, gloves

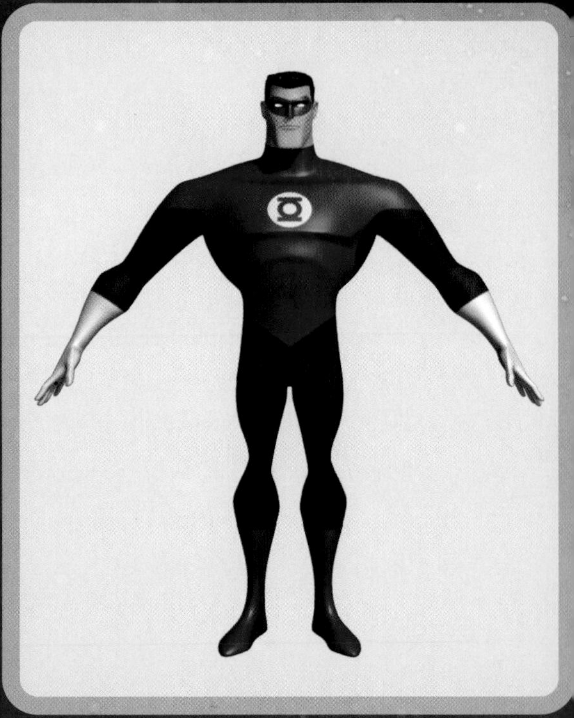

4.) Fill in the colors with crayons or markers

CREATORS

ART BALTAZAR *writer*

Art Baltazar is a cartoonist machine from the heart of Chicago! He defines cartoons and comics not only as an art style, but as a way of life. Currently, Art is the creative force behind *The New York Times* best-selling, Eisner Award-winning, DC Comics series Tiny Titans, and the co-writer for *Billy Batson and the Magic of SHAZAM!* and co-creator of the Superman Family Adventures series. Art is living the dream! He draws comics and never has to leave the house. He lives with his lovely wife, Rose, big boy Sonny, little boy Gordon, and little girl Audrey. Right on!

FRANCO AURELIANI *writer*

Bronx, New York born writer and artist Franco Aureliani has been drawing comics since he could hold a crayon. Currently residing in upstate New York with his wife, Ivette, and son, Nicolas, Franco spends most of his days in a Batcave-like studio where he produces DC's Tiny Titans comics. In 1995, Franco founded Blindwolf Studios, an independent art studio where he and fellow creators can create children's comics. Franco is the creator, artist, and writer of *Weirdsville*, *L'il Creeps*, and *Eagle All Star*, as well as the co-creator and writer of *Patrick the Wolf Boy*. When he's not writing and drawing, Franco also teaches high school art.

DARIO BRIZUELA *illustrator*

Dario Brizuela is a professional comic book artist. He's illustrated some of today's most popular characters, including Batman, Green Lantern, Teenage Mutant Ninja Turtles, Thor, Iron Man, and Transformers. His best-known works for DC Comics include the series DC Super Friends, Justice League Unlimited, and Batman: The Brave and the Bold.

GLOSSARY

cavalry (KAV-uhl-ree) — troops mounted on horseback or moving in motor vehicles or helicopters

civilized (SIV-ih-lyzd) — an advanced stage of social development, as shown by manners and education

contradict (kon-truh-DIKT) — to say the opposite of what has been said

evac (EE-vak) — an abbreviation for "evacuate," to remove troops or people from a place of danger

maim (MAYM) — to injure or disfigure badly

marshal (MAR-shuhl) — a federal official having duties similar to those of a sheriff

proximity (prok-SIM-uh-tee) — nearness

rage (RAYJ) — very strong and uncontrolled anger

scenario (suh-NAIR-ee-oh) — an outline of a series of events that might happen in a particular situation

VISUAL QUESTIONS

1. With his powerful green ring, Hal Jordan can create anything he imagines. If you wore a power ring, what would you create? Why?

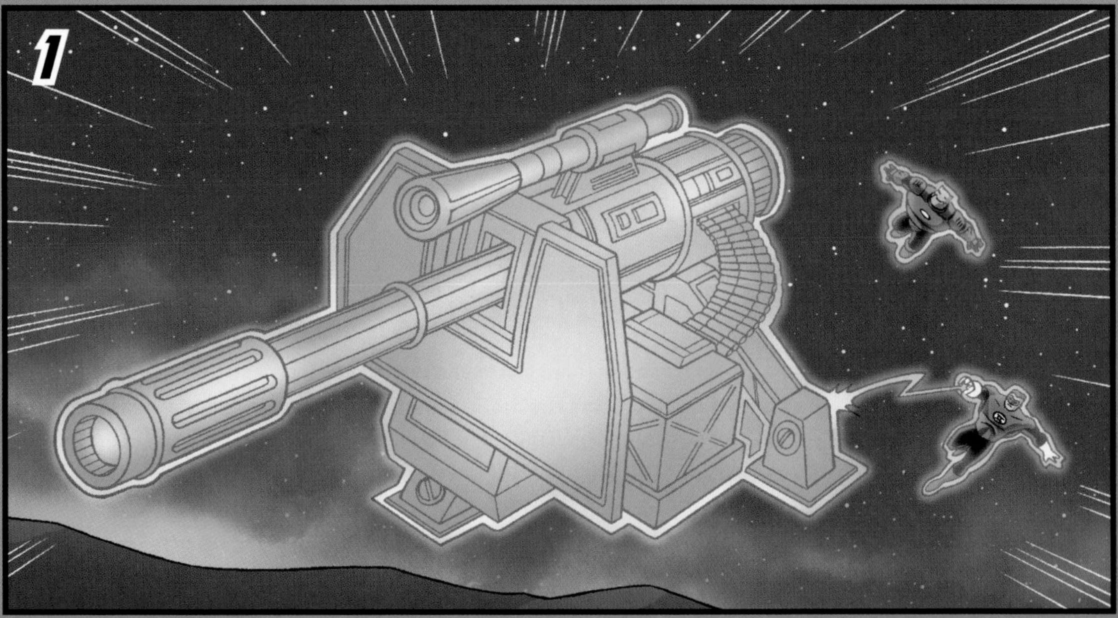
1

2. In comic books, much of the story is told through the illustrations. Describe what is happening in the two wordless panels below, from page 13. How does Kilowog manage to escape the Red Lanterns?

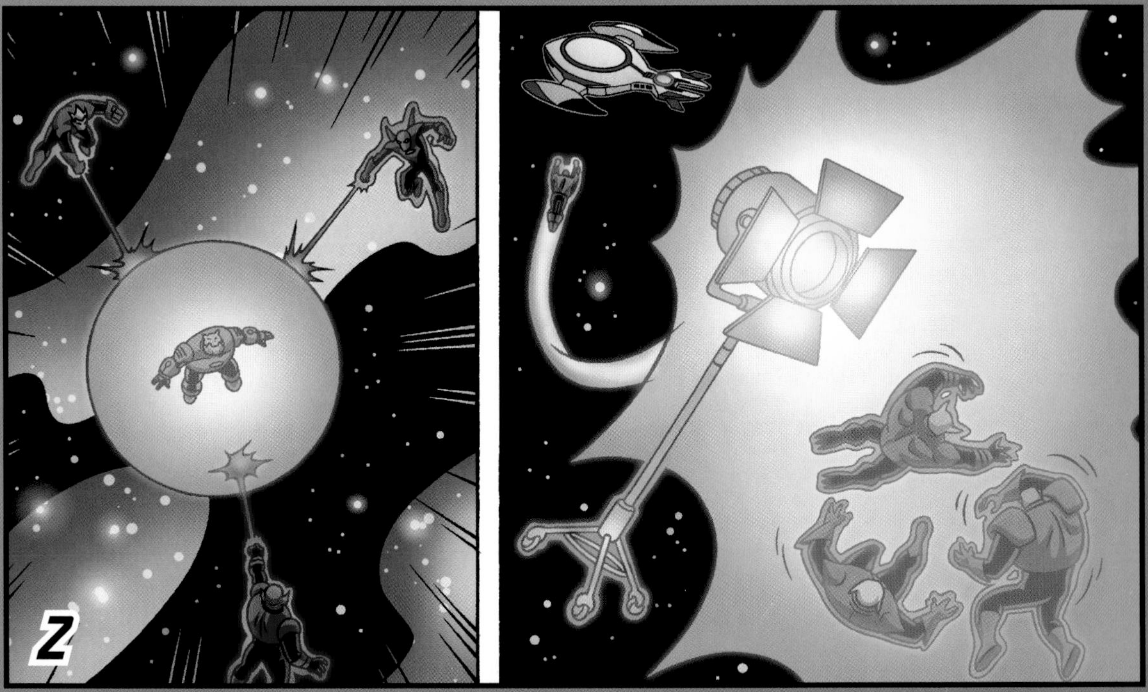
2

3. Many different colors of power rings are scattered throughout the universe. Green power rings are fueled by willpower. Red rings are powered by rage. Create your own ring. What color is it? What emotion powers your ring, and why?

4. Members of the Green Lantern Corps work together to protect the universe. Look back through this book, and find at least two examples of Hal Jordan and Kilowog helping each other. Do you think either of them could have defeated the Red Lanterns alone?

5. The way a character's eyes and mouth look, also known as their facial expression, can tell a lot about the emotions he or she is feeling. At left, how do you think Hal Jordan is feeling? Why?

READ THEM ALL!

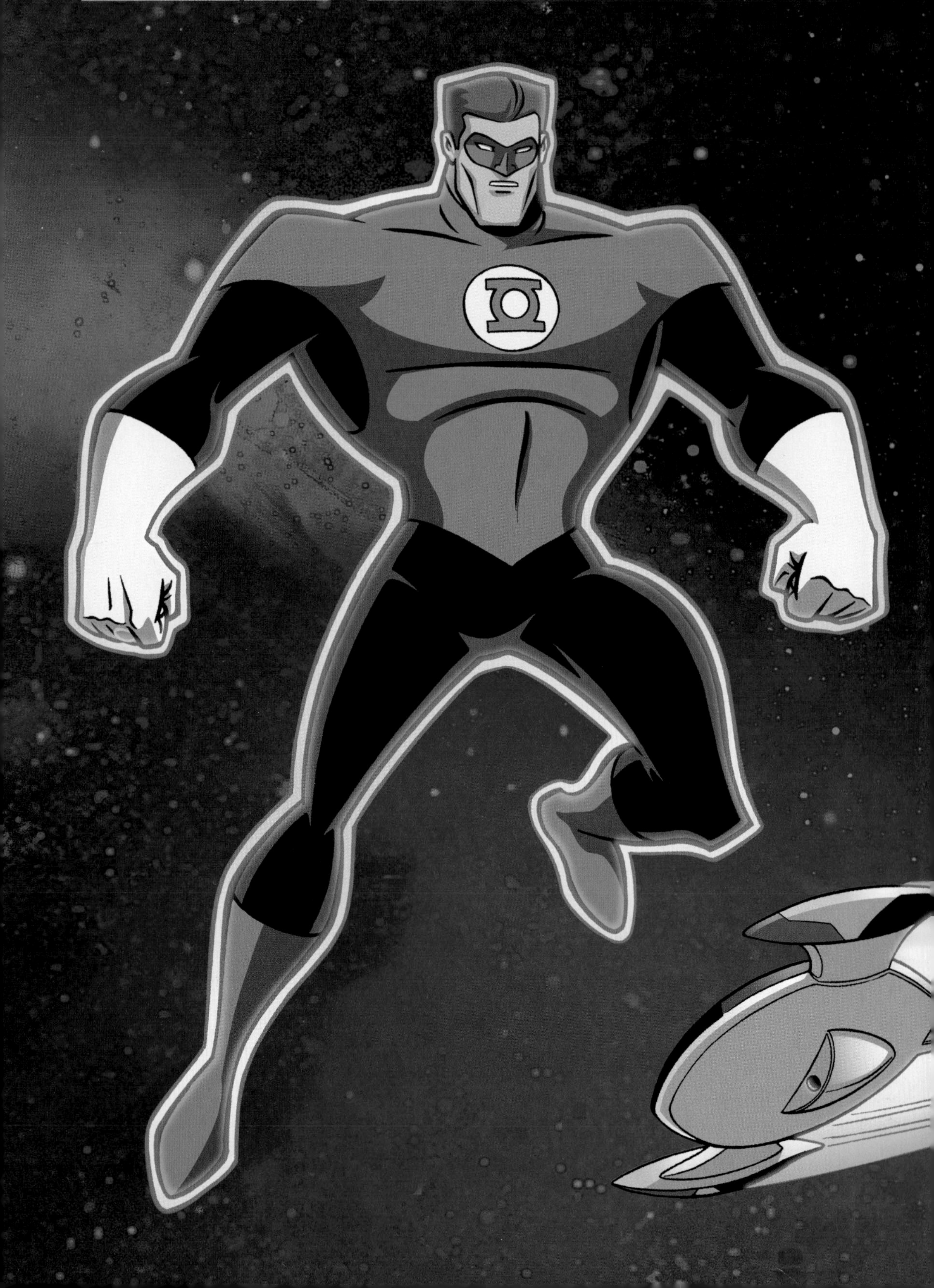

GREEN LANTERN

THE ANIMATED SERIES™

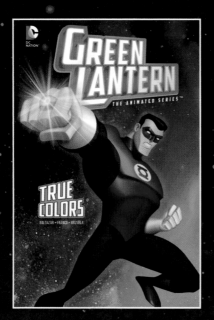

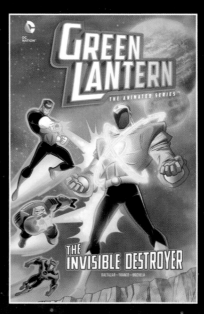

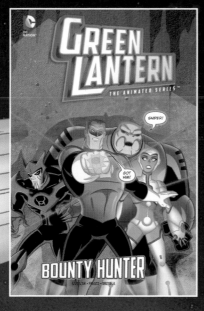

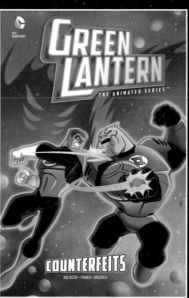

only from...

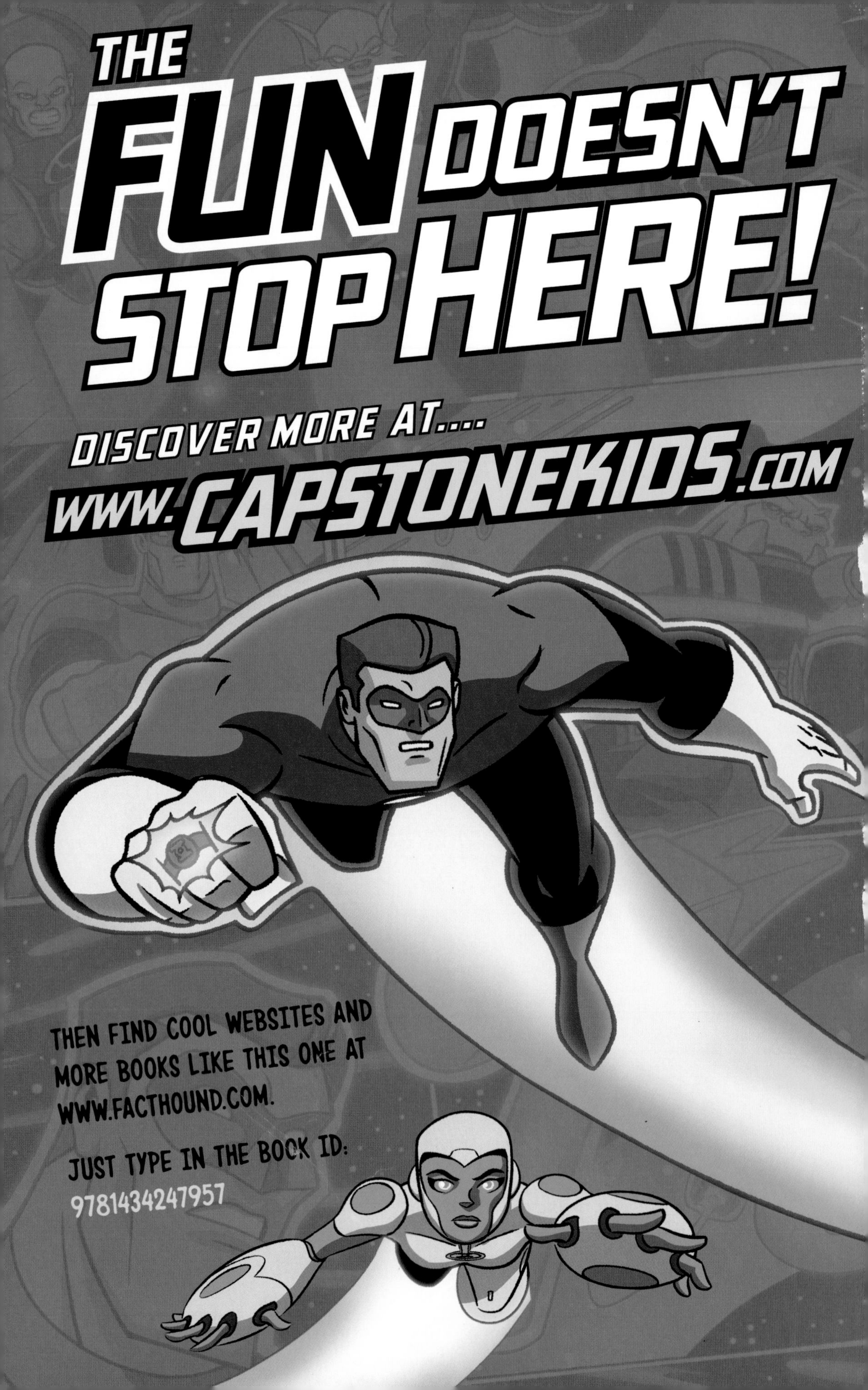
THE FUN DOESN'T STOP HERE!
DISCOVER MORE AT....
WWW.CAPSTONEKIDS.COM
THEN FIND COOL WEBSITES AND MORE BOOKS LIKE THIS ONE AT WWW.FACTHOUND.COM.
JUST TYPE IN THE BOOK ID:
9781434247957